"What kind of woman are you underneath?"

Tyler continued softly, "Are you really the shy innocent who's wary of a holiday romance? Or are you what those snapping green eyes keep promising?"

Laurie stared up at him. Why did this puzzling man keep doubting that she was anything other than what she seemed?

"We could have something going and you know it," he was saying as he drew her closer.

Laurie swallowed nervously. "I—I don't even know if I like you," she stammered.

"You don't have to like me," came the husky reply. "But you can't deny the attraction that's between us."

She wanted to resist him, but words of denial just wouldn't come. And before she could move his mouth was on hers, and he was kissing her passionately....

But Know Not Why

by

JESSICA STEELE

Harlequin Books

TORONTO • LONDON • LOS ANGELES • AMSTERDAM
SYDNEY • HAMBURG • PARIS • STOCKHOLM • ATHENS • TOKYO

Original hardcover edition published in 1982
by Mills & Boon Limited

ISBN 0-373-02494-0

Harlequin Romance first edition August 1982

CHAPTER ONE

LAURIE FROST breezed through the main entrance of Craye & Company that Monday in January and thought she could be forgiven if her mind wandered that day. Mustn't get too excited, she thought, as she tripped lightly up the stairs to her first floor office. She had three whole working days to get through yet before she and Kay took that plane in the direction of the Far East early on Thursday morning.

Kay was looking forward to their holiday as much as she was, she thought happily, as she tried to keep down the bubble of anticipation that wanted to rise to the surface again. It had been the main topic of conversation ever since Mei Lai had mooted the idea when between them they had taken the Hong Kong Chinese girl around London those couple of weeks last year.

Laurie came out of her reverie to see she had nearly missed seeing Alastair Yardley, head bent, shoulders slightly stooped for all he couldn't be much more than forty.

'Good morning, Professor,' she called as she passed him, but she needn't have bothered, for as frequently was the case he was on another planet and hadn't seen her, much less heard her.

A grin tugged, curved upwards her mouth that just missed being perfectly shaped by having a slightly fuller bottom lip. She guessed Alastair, Craye & Co.'s tame research physicist, was too deep in thought with the erosion problem he had been working on for what must be months now. A problem he had declared would give them a lead over their many rivals all over the world—if only he could crack it.

'Morning, Maurice,' she called, going into her office and seeing her boss Maurice Lancaster through the open door, his desk already starting to look the pigsty it would by the end of the day.

'You needn't sound so cheerful,' he returned, lifting his fair head and looking at her throught his black-framed glasses that didn't make him look a year older than his thirty-two years. 'Morning, Laurie,' he thought to add.

'Ah—never mind,' she said, shedding her coat and going in to him. 'It's not all bad news, is it?' knowing his remark was because he would shortly be without her fairly efficient self for three weeks. 'Anona will be coming to fill in for me as she did last year, and I know of the two of us whom you'd rather have around all day.'

Maurice was too gallant to agree, but she saw the smile that came to his features as she reminded him that his ex-secretary, now his wife, would be occupying her chair from Thursday.

'Yes, well, let's make a start, shall we?'

Fully occupied as she was that morning, Laurie still found time to let her mind wander. It hadn't done with thinking about her holiday when her thoughts flitted on to Anona Lancaster.

There had been no need for Anona to work at all, even before she had given up her job on marrying Maurice, for her brother was head of the prosperous firm and open-handed with his sister. Though Laurie was glad Anona had decided eighteen months ago that even with the live-in help she had, the large house she and Maurice had moved into, combined with their busy social life, was still too much to manage and keep on with her job. For it had let her in, and she had taken to the job like a duck to water.

Not that it was everybody's cup of tea, she mused, her fingers busy on her typewriter, her mind momentarily coming away from T. Harcourt Craye's sister. But she loved it. Maurice was in charge of the administration side of the research and development department specially set up some years ago. And for all much of the work she did, figures she typed that were so much Greek to her for all she could understand them, there was such an air of camaraderie between the whole section, it more than made up for the occasional patches of boredom that were common to most people's careers.

She checked what she had just typed and saw that even with only half her concentration on her work it was accurate. Then she inserted a fresh sheet of quarto in her machine and was off again, her mind this time flitting to T. Harcourt Craye, the boss of the whole shoot, but whom because he had swanky offices the other side of town she had never seen. She could have done on two occasions, though—she halted her flow. He had come to see the Professor about something about a year ago. That had been the time she had been too ill with 'flu to drag herself to the office.

The other time had been the day six months ago when she had had the day off to take Mei Lai sightseeing. It had been the time when Maurice, for all he thought the world of Anona, had gone off the rails and had a brief affair. Laurie had never been able to understand quite what had got into him, loving his wife as he did, but she thought that maybe he had been flattered by the attention he received in a social circle new to him after his marriage.

Being in such close contact with him daily, Laurie had known more than anyone that Maurice was playing around. He knew she knew it too, for all she had tried to keep her feelings hidden when she had overheard him sending his girl-friend flowers and the gooey message that went with them.

But it had frightened him when he had come to his senses and realised he stood to lose Anona. And maybe because he needed a listening ear, knowing from the confidential work they did that Laurie could keep her mouth closed, he had told her not only about his affair, but that Anona had found out about it and had told her brother.

He had also told her about the visit he had had from Anona's brother, T. Harcourt Craye, and how he had come gunning for him.

'I thought he was going to murder me,' Maurice, still looking peaky from the experience, had told her next day. 'He's twelve years older than Anona and has looked out for her since their parents died. He wiped the floor with me, I don't mind telling you, letting me know without pulling his punches that if it wasn't for the fact that Anona still loved me I'd be joining the dole queue.'

Not knowing what she could say to that, for the way Maurice was saying it, T. Harcourt Craye sounded a terrifying man to upset, Laurie had tried to look sympathetic, for all most of her sympathy was for Anona.

'Maybe it was because he could see I was ready to take anything he dished out, but that it was killing me that I'd irresponsibly hurt my dear wife so, that Harcourt didn't beat me to a pulp, but settled for giving me the worst dressing down of my life,' Maurice had gone on, seeming to feel the need to talk it out of his system. 'I'll tell you this much, though, Laurie—with or without his threats of what he'll do to me if I dare to hurt her again, I just wouldn't. The whole thing has made me realise I love Anona more than I knew, makes me feel ill inside that I've caused her a moment's distress.'

Laurie finished her typing and went out to lunch musing that all was set fair in the Lancaster camp now. For Anona had forgiven him and from what she had seen of them together on the occasions Anona had come to the office, two turtle doves wasn't overstating it.

But her belief that her boss and his wife were now enjoying a better relationship than they had ever done dipped during the afternoon when she went in to see Maurice for some figures he wanted typing. She was just about to rise after he had handed her the papers he had sorted from the conglomeration of paper work on his desk when she saw from his expression that he wanted to ask her something.

'If you want me to bring you back one of those flat ducks from Hong Kong, the answer's no,' she told him, having been regaled during the waiting minutes of him searching among his papers on the ducks that he had seen the last time he had been in Hong Kong hanging up on market stalls, flattened, so he said, so that they couldn't be more than an inch thick.

Maurice chuckled. 'Wouldn't dream of it,' he said. 'Though I do have a favour to ask you.'

Laurie really couldn't spare the time to work late, she hadn't started her packing yet. 'For you, Maurice—anything,' she said, wondering if she would be packing her case a couple of hours before the plane took off.

But the favour he had to ask had nothing to do with overtime, as he revealed that everything between him and Anona was not nearly as back to normal as she had thought.

'It's Anona's birthday four weeks tomorrow,' he began. 'And after racking my brains for something extra special for her I hit on something she'll be ecstatic over.'

Laurie smiled, seeing for herself that Maurice was having enormous pleasure from just anticipating Anona's delight. 'What have you got her?' she asked, not seeing how this could have anything to do with the favour he was asking. 'Or do you want to keep it a secret?'

'Secret from Anona,' he answered, going to to tell her about a family ring that had been handed down which Anona loved but no longer wore because one of the stones was missing. 'It was loose the last time she wore it and had gone when we got home,' he said, 'so I've had a new diamond set in for her birthday.'

'Oh, Maurice—how lovely!' Laurie exclaimed. 'She'll be delighted.'

'She will,' he agreed, then, his face sobering, 'The thing is, though, I can't take it home yet because I don't want her to see it until her birthday morning.'

'Can't you hide it somewhere?' Laurie queried, remembering childhood Christmases when presents had been hidden in the most ingenious of places by her parents. Then she saw her question had made her boss look more than a shade uncomfortable.

'Er—since that—er—business six months ago,' he said, his embarrassment showing, 'since I shattered Anona's feeling of security—God, I must have been mad!—well, you can't really blame her, but she's taken to—er—poking about in my things.'

Startled by this revelation, Laurie's first thought was, poor Anona, her trust in Maurice must have taken a gigantic blow that she was still checking for evidence of another woman. And poor Maurice, she thought, knowing just how hard he was trying to make up for what he had done. Then the sadness of what he had revealed was ousted, surprise taking it as it dawned on her what the favour he wanted must be.

'You want me to keep the ring for you?' she questioned, unable to keep the surprise from her voice.

'Would you?' he asked eagerly.

'But—but I'm going away!' she exclaimed, wanting to help, sure Anona would be thrilled with her present, but not wanting the responsibility of the ring. He had said he had had a diamond set in it. And if the ring had belonged to the wealthy Craye family then it was bound to be worth a bomb even without that stone.

'That's all right,' he said, suddenly cheerful now that his confidences were out of the way.

'But I can't leave a valuable item like that lying around,' she protested, sure it must be worth a mint when Maurice didn't disclaim that it was valuable.

'Oh, come on, Laurie! How many times have you been burgled in the last four years?'

'Well, none,' she admitted, having four years ago at the age of eighteen left her comfortable home in Warwick to try her wings in London. And following Maurice's train of thought she knew he was thinking the area he lived was far more likely to have night time visitors than in her less well-to-do area.

'There you are, then,' he proclaimed, as though as far as he was concerned the matter was settled.

'Can't you leave it at the jewellers until nearer the time?' she tried, still wanting to help, but hoping he would see she felt the responsibility of the article went beyond the call of duty.

'They're moving into new premises at the weekend,' he told her. 'I don't want any last-minute foul-ups in the shape of it being temporarily mislaid in the change-over.'

To her way of thinking any arrangements the jewellers made would be well thought out in view of their cargo. But she could see Maurice was begining to look anxious.

'Please, Laurie, do this for me. I've been saving up for ages to afford to do this out of my own money. Harcourt is more than generous to us, but I wanted to pay for Anona's present out of my own pocket.'

That got to her quicker than anything else he could have said. 'When are you picking it up?' she asked, knowing the legs of objection had just been knocked from under her.

'On Wednesday. You can take it home, put it somewhere out of the way and forget about it until you come back from your holiday.' Maurice was all smiles. 'All you have to do then is bring it with you to work four weeks today ready for me to take home on Monday night.'

Laurie was plagued by conscience for the rest of the afternoon. While still not liking to have the ring at her flat, she couldn't help but feel a meanie at having objected in the first place when Anona would feel so much joy at what Maurice had done for her. And he was right, of course, she was fairly certain she could leave her flat unlocked and no one would so much as bother to try the door.

She was in Maurice's office sorting a mound of papers

from his desk into their correct files to be put away neatly before she went home, when Alastair Yardley came in with yet more paper work.

'Made your break through yet, Alastair?' Maurice asked him, casually handing Laurie the key to the safe so she could lock the Professor's work away for the night.

'Ask me in six months' time,' said Alastair dourly. Then, aware of the lovely redhead he had missed seeing that morning, he handed her his papers, saying, 'A few of us from the lab are going for a jar—fancy coming with us?'

'Not tonight, thanks, Alastair,' Laurie refused, having gone a few times with the gang for an after-work half while they unwound and cleared their heads of whatever scientific matter went on up there. 'I have masses to do,' and since she didn't think he would remember, she trotted out, trying not to show off, 'I'm going to Hong Kong on Thursday.'

'That's soon come round,' he replied, when she had been counting the days for months now. He dug into his memory. 'Aren't you taking in China as well?'

'Starting the second week, but only for six days,' she answered, thinking to tone it down a bit in case it had sounded as though she was showing off. 'And then only thanks to Mei Lai.'

Maurice filled in for her on seeing that Alastair was trying to look as though he knew what she was talking about when clearly he didn't. 'Mei Lai is that beautiful little Chinese girl who works for a company we deal with in Hong Kong. She popped in to see us when she was over here last July, and since she and Laurie got on so well she's insisted that Laurie stays with her.'

'So what has this Mei Lai to do with the China bit?' asked the Professor, who was nothing short of brilliant at his job, but whose comprehension in other fields was a touch limited.

Sure she had already told him, Laurie joined in to re-tell him, 'Had I been going to stay in a hotel in Hong Kong I would never been able to have afforded the China tour.'

'Ah, I see,' said the Professor. 'Well, don't forget to bring me back a stick of rock.'

Laurie's lips were still twitching at Alastair's remark when she went home. After her meal, judging that her friend Kay would have eaten too, she picked up the phone to give her a ring. Since Kay didn't have a phone of her own Laurie had a few minutes to wait while someone went and fetched her to the communal phone in the hall, excitement threatening to overflow as she waited.

But her excitement changed to concern when Kay eventually came to the phone, for her friend was nowhere near as bubbling over with the same excitement that had been in her voice the last time Laurie had spoken with her.

'What's the matter?' she asked at once.

'Nothing I can put my finger on. I just feel—yuk!' Kay answered, already starting to sound brighter. 'Not to worry, though, I shall be all right by tomorrow. Probably the stodge of canteen food getting to me. Have you packed yet?'

'Have I ever! Going to make a start in a minute.'

With Kay picking up the longer they chatted, Laurie's concern for her friend faded. And anticipation was there in both their voices as they reminisced on the time last year when they had both done their best to ensure that Mei Lai had an enjoyable time, and they re-checked their arrangements.

'Neither Mei Lai nor her mother will be there the first week, will they?' Kay checked again, having like Laurie had many things to see to, travel arrangements, money, visa, and purchases to make specially for the holiday, so she could be forgiven for getting confused.

'That's right,' Laurie confirmed, being the one who had recently heard from their Far East friend. 'Mei Lai's grandmother is quite poorly in mainland China, so Mrs Wong has already left to go and see her and will stay as long as she's needed. But Mei Lai can't have more than a week off work, so she'll be haring off to join her mother on the Friday we arrive. That means, unfortunately, that we won't see Mei Lai until we return from China ourselves.'

'Pity we can't meet up with her there,' opined Kay. 'Though with us setting off for China a week the following Saturday, we'll probably pass her in transit if she has to be back at work on the Monday.'

After her call to Kay, Laurie got down to some serious packing, sadly having to discard one or two items when a test run on her case showed that with the last-minute things she had to put in, it was never going to close.

Tuesday was a hectic day at work, making her feel in need of her holiday as prior to going to bed that night she sat brushing her naturally wavy shoulder-length hair. But there was still that excited shine to be seen in her large green eyes as she thought of arriving in Hong Kong, of actually being there!

She had telephoned Kay earlier and heard her friend saying she felt fine again, Kay, like her, trying to keep the lid down on her excitement.

Wednesday was less hectic, with Laurie taking time off during the course of the morning to hope, when glancing through the jumble Maurice had already made of his desk—for all he always said he knew where everything was—that in her absence Anona as his temporary secretary might be able to do what she had been unable to achieve, and have him trained in better ways by the time she returned.

It was the middle of the afternoon, when having done everything she could possibly think of doing to leave things respectable for her successor, that she went in to see Maurice to clear up a few loose ends. He invited her to sit down, so she knew that since he had worked hard too that he was ready for a break.

She wasn't surprised when he pulled the small square ring box out of his pocket and placed it on top of some papers on his desk. He had said he was collecting Anona's ring today.

'There it is,' he announced. 'Thanks a million, Laurie.'

'Can I have a look?' she asked—then she was gasping as he lifted back the lid. 'Maurice, I can't possibly leave anything as valuable as this lying around in my flat!' she exclaimed without hesitation as the unusually set emerald and diamond antique ring winked back at her. 'It'd look well if . . .'

'Oh, for goodness' sake!' Maurice countered, rarely irritable, endorsing by his irritability how much it meant to him that his wife was totally surprised.

But Laurie was too panicky at the thought that someone might break into her flat while she was away to let his tone worry her too much. The emerald alone would keep her in luxury for a year.

'Leave it in the office safe, Maurice,' she urged. 'It will be far safer . . .'

'How can I, with Anona working here?' he sliced through her argument. 'You know as well as I do that in an absentminded moment I'm just as likely to hand her the safe key when anything wants putting away. I do it with you all the time—leave it with you sometimes. Besides, I couldn't hurt her feelings by closing my door, shutting her out, every time Alastair comes in with something for the safe.'

Although she did not feel very happy about it, at last Laurie was persuaded against her better judgment to go and put the ring in her handbag. And returning, she saw that Maurice was doing all he could to atone for his irritation with her as he endeavoured to lift her spirits by begining a conversation about the last time he had been in Hong Kong.

'You'll love it,' he told her. 'The scenery is fabulous, particularly in the New Territories.' Managing a smile, Laurie did feel herself begin to grow more cheerful as he explained that the archipelago was made up of Hong Kong Island, Kowloon Peninsular, the New Territories and about two hundred and thirty odd outlying islands. 'It'll be warm there too at this time of year,' he said. 'Lucky you, to escape our English climate in January.'

Work was forgotten as he told her about the New Year celebrations which started early in February, but which she would miss; of the flower markets when the whole of Hong Kong turned out at midnight, or so it had seemed.

He snapped his fingers, something he had a habit of doing when a thought suddenly came to him. 'I've just remembered, there's a fabulous restaurant in the Wanchai district. You must go there, Laurie. Now what was it called . . .'

But before he could have time to think about it the outer door burst open and the Professor was hurrying in, his face more animated than Laurie had ever seen it, a smile splitting his face like a wedge of melon.

There was no need for him to tell them that something pretty momentous had happened, it was there in his face. But having got as far as Maurice's desk, Alastair seemed lost for words, and just stood there waving the sheaf of papers in his hand.

'You've cracked it?' Maurice guessed, his voice quietly hushed. 'You've solved that metal erosion problem.'

Alastair's smile grew wider than ever. 'By pure chance,' he said jubilantly, talking rapidly now that he had found his voice. 'For months now I've been plodding away, checking, re-checking, then for some unknown reason my mind wandered into a totally irrelevant channel . . .' he paused as thought he still couldn't believe it, '. . . and—there it was!'

Maurice was out of his chair in a flash, warmly wringing the Professor's hand, Laurie too was on her feet congratulating him. Talk then became scientifically technical as Alastair explained the whys and wherefores, which went right over her head. From the glazed look in Maurice's eyes, she guessed he too was having difficulty in assimilating all that was being said, even though he was nodding his head as though he understood. But she couldn't help but be happy for Alastair that his months of hard work had paid off, vaguely remembering something from school about how Sir Alexander Fleming's discovery of penicillin had come about from something that had appeared quite irrelevant.

She picked up the conversation again when Alastair had left off his technical explanations and was asking Maurice if he had any idea where he might be able to contact Harcourt. 'He'll want to be here as soon as he hears my news,' he said confidently, his spirits never higher.

Laurie knew from Maurice that T. Harcourt Craye was something of a mathematician himself, and she didn't doubt that he would have more understanding of the breakthrough the Professor had made than she and Maurice. And she silently agreed, while she rejoiced for Alastair, that the big boss would be over as soon as he heard.

'He's flying in from Argentina today,' Maurice told him. 'He could be at his office or at home by now.'

'I'll go and give him a ring.' Alastair's excitement had him half out of the door before he came back and placed his papers on the desk. 'You'd better put these in the safe,' he said. 'They're vitally important. It wouldn't do for them to get into the wrong hands before Harcourt gets here.'

Laurie's smile broadened as he went out as she wondered if their tame professor thought some industrial spy was lurking in the corridor waiting for just this moment to mug him. Thinking the importance of the papers called for a new file all of their own, she went and found one. Maurice's thoughts were on the same wave length as hers as he handed the papers over for her to slip inside before he gave her the key and watched while she locked them in the safe.

Unable to get back to work straight away, because the Professor's elation had rubbed off on to both of them, they discussed how Alastair had deserved his success.

'Harcourt will get the champagne out over this, make no mistake,' said Maurice. 'Notwithstanding the handsome financial award that will be going Alastair's way,' adding by the way, 'They've known each other from their university days.'

Laurie pondered this piece of information. Maurice had told her Anona's brother was twelve years older than her. That meant that since Anona was twenty-four—twenty-five in a month's time—then he must be thirty-six or thirty-seven. Yet Maurice was saying he and the Professor were contemporaries.

'I thought the Professor was over forty?' she said.

'He worries a lot,' quipped Maurice, thinking to tack on, 'Don't let him hear you say that!'

Laurie grinned, then Maurice was asking what they were doing before Alastair had burst in.

'Tying up loose ends, I think,' she said, steering her mind back to work. 'Oh, and you were going to give me the address of that restaurant in Hong Kong.'

He found a piece of paper from the mound on his desk, thought for about a minute, then in his large untidy print that very near filled a quarto sheet, quickly wrote down the address and gave it to her.

She studied the address, which meant nothing to her.

Then while she went to tuck it away in an unused compartment of her large wallet-type purse—making a mental note to transfer it to her Hong Kong wallet-cum-purse later since this one was large enough not to get her English and Chinese currency mixed up, but would be confusing if she had all three currencies in it—Maurice went out. Probably to see if Alastair had contacted T. Harcourt Craye, she thought.

Maurice was back at five when she put the cover over her typewriter, her mind already on her flight tomorrow morning. She wouldn't be seeing her typewriter for another three and a half weeks; and she wasn't bothered in the slightest about that.

'Have a good holiday, Laurie,' he said, coming through. 'Lord knows you've earned it, putting up with me all this time.'

'Oh, you're not so bad,' she teased him—then saw that instead of smiling at her sauce as he would normally have done, he was suddenly very serious. Serious and a shade emotional.

'I can't thank you enough for keeping that ring safe for me,' he said. 'Anona's going to be over the moon.'

'It's a pleasure,' she said, purely because there was nothing else she could have said.

'Thank you, my dear,' he said sincerely. And, his emotion being on top of him at that moment, he added a kiss on her cheek to his thanks.

Thinking that perhaps he was more of a sensitive man than she had realised, Laurie could not find the 'Don't be daft' that needed to be said. But oh, how she wished she had when she moved to pick up her bag and saw that, unheard by either of them, the outer door had opened and Anona stood there, the wounded look on her face showing she had seen Maurice's peck on her cheek and misinterpreted it.

'Maurice was just—wishing me a happy holiday,' she

said lamely, hating that she felt defensive.

'So I see,' Anona remarked coolly, and turned sharply about, just as Maurice was exclaiming:

'Anona—darling!' and went charging after her.

Oh hell, Laurie thought, wondering if it would do any good if she hung about. Anona hadn't made off in the direction of the exit, so she had probably headed for the ladies' cloakroom.

Deciding that at that precise moment she would most likely be a red rag to Anona if Maurice hadn't been able to pacify her, for since he wanted the ring kept darkly secret he wouldn't be able to tell his wife what that peck on the cheek had been all about, Laurie gathered up her things, her mood of holiday happiness gone as she made her way to the stairs.

Her mind full of Maurice trying to placate his wife, she turned the corner and went smack bang into the large man rounding the same bend.

'Look where you're going!' he ordered her churlishly, and was going up the stairs two at a time before she had so much as glimpsed his face, black hair and a broad back all she could see of him.

Ignorant devil! she thought, as she swung through the door, a large opulent car drawn up at the entrance that was supposed to be kept clear. She was in her car driving home when it came to her that since the man she had dubbed 'ignorant devil' seemed to think he had every right to park wherever he wanted, apart from the fact that nobody who worked in the building owned a car like *that*, then the man who had told her to look where she was going could be none other than T. Harcourt Craye himself.

Thinking she had lost nothing by missing seeing him the two times he had deigned to visit his other premises, Laurie drove on. She had been home an hour or two when she finally decided that by now Anona and Maurice would have sorted themselves out, then she promptly forgot about them and the ignorant T. Harcourt Craye, thoughts of her journey tomorrow being far more exciting.

At eight o'clock she first telephoned her parents, then with her father's advice to 'be careful' realised he still thought of her as his baby girl, and thought to give Kay a ring to check that she had no last-minute panics.

But to her consternation, the girl who answered the phone told her Kay wasn't around, that she had last been seen that morning being taken away in an ambulance.

'Ambulance? What . . .'

'Oh, nothing serious,' came the airy information. 'Just appendicitis, that's all.'

That the tenant in Kay's block seemed to think appendicitis fell into the same category as having a splinter removed was mind-boggling enough without anything else. But quickly getting over her shock, Laurie asked which hospital Kay had been taken to, learned it was one miles away, and having nothing more to say to the person who seemed to have little time for illness, she thanked her very much and hung up.

She had hunted up the telephone number of the hospital before it came to her that Kay was going to feel even more ghastly than was usual with appendicitis at the thought that her holiday had gone up in smoke. The hospital were far more likely to let her see her if she presented herself on the doorstep than if she rang up and asked for permission.

Without another thought, she grabbed up her coat and bag, and was tearing out of the house, her eyes barely registering the stranger to the street in the shape of a Ford Cortina not far from her car.

It was maybe because Kay was in a tearful state, visiting hour having long since gone by the time Laurie, having taken several wrong turnings, got to the hospital, that she was allowed in to see her.

'Oh, Laurie, thank heavens you got my message! I thought Susan had forgotten to ring you when you didn't come at visiting time,' said the blonde-haired Kay, and, her pale face crumpling, 'I'm so s-sorry.'

Laurie guessed that whoever Susan was, she had been meant to tell her of her friend's illness, but she didn't think it would do Kay any good to know her message hadn't been delivered.

'You couldn't help it,' she tried to soothe her. And, trying to get a smile from her, 'I don't suppose you went down with appendicitis on purpose!'

It had the desired effect, for all the smile Kay offered was a weak one. 'You'll still go, won't you?' she asked, when Laurie had come to no firm decision about it yet. 'Oh, do say you'll go! I shall feel worse than ever if because of me your holiday is ruined too.'

'Of course I'll go,' Laurie told her swiftly. 'It won't be the same, but . . .'

'You'll be all right, Laurie,' Kay promised, knowing better than anyone outside her family that Laurie had an inbuilt sense of misdirection, which had caused her nightmares when she had first moved to London. 'Mei Lai said you can't possible get lost in Hong Kong, and if you do, all you have to do is follow the tram tracks. And besides, you'll have Mei Lai for company on the third week—in the evenings, anyhow.'

She was allowed to stay with Kay for fifteen minutes before a nurse came and politely told her Miss Richards should rest now, though looking pleased that her patient, still a trifle woebegone, appeared much less tearful now than she had done.

Getting into her car, Laurie thought she must be imagining things, that the same Cortina she had glimpsed outside her flat was standing parked not very far away from hers.

She forgot about it as she set her car in motion, and concentrated all her navigational powers on getting home without ending up in too many blind alleys.

Knowing she was committed to going on her holiday, but with some of the joy gone since Kay wouldn't be accompanying her, she let herself into her flat intending to rearrange her suitcase a little to allow for her toilet bag in the morning, have a quick bath and go to bed.

But it was as she opened her suitcase and saw that the sweater she had placed on top was all out of alignment, and lying there not at all in the neat way it was second nature to her to lay out her things, that the hairs on the back of her neck began to prickle.

Alarmed, she straightened up. Straightened up and turned slowly round the room—then froze. Someone had been in her flat—she knew it! Fear hit her as, not wanting to believe it, she investigated the kitchen and her bedroom.

Relief about to rush in that her imagination was playing tricks with her, for everything looked normal, she glanced towards the bed—and alarm was with her again, intensified. She had *never* left her bed with the bottom sheet dangling like that! Nausea was added to her alarm. Nausea that some criminal had touched the bed she was to sleep in.

She conquered her fear and her nausea as she made her mind search for a reason why anybody should break into her flat. Why disturb her bed, lift up the mattress, by the look of it? The only thing she had of value was the gold chain her parents had given her for her twenty-first birthday, and she was wearing that. Oh!

Oh no! Laurie thought, having forgotten all about the ring in her dash to see Kay. It must be the ring! Maurice must have told somebody she was keeping it for him, that somebody could have told somebody else, anybody . . .!

She needed to sit down, her nerves were so shaken,

but she first of all checked her handbag to see she still had the ring. It sparkled back at her, was beautiful and valuable, and she knew then there was only thing she could do.

Her eyes flew to the clock. Half past eleven. A bit late to ring Maurice at home, but he'd have to come and collect it, meet her at the airport tomorrow or something—she just couldn't leave it here for any petty criminal to get his hands on. Maurice must have been off his head to suggest such a thing.

Quickly she dialled his number, heard a voice that wasn't his answer. 'Can I speak to Maurice—Mr Lancaster?' she asked the male voice. And because of the lateness of the hour and whoever it was might have to drag Maurice out of bed, too strung up about her intruder to remember that Anona had clearly thought something was going on between her and Maurice, 'Would you tell him it's Laurie.'

There was a pause, so she thought the man had gone away to get Maurice to the phone. Then she found he hadn't budged. And not only that, but that his voice had changed, was rude like that man she had bumped into coming out of Craye & Co. And added to that, it was biting with aggression, as he snarled:

'You've got one hell of a nerve—don't you see enough of your lover without having the *bloody cheek* to ring him at my sister's home?'

Laurie could hardly believe it as the phone went crashing down in her ear. She stared dumbfounded at the receiver in her hand—and still couldn't believe it.

CHAPTER TWO

HONG KONG Laurie found entirely fascinating. Being nervous of finding her way around on her own at first, she had spent the first week or so of her holiday exploring, gradually becoming more and more adventurous.

Yesterday, for instance, she mused as she sat in the train that was taking her and her tour group from the mainland China border to Canton, she had hopped on a tram, crossed to Kowloon on the ferry, and had eventually caught a bus to spend a most enjoyable day exploring part of the New Territories.

And still there was that feeling of excitement in her. It didn't seem possible that she, Lauretta Frost, who was apt to lose her way if she didn't keep her wits about her, should actually be sitting alone in a train travelling in China!

She glanced down the centre aisle of the comfortable first class compartment, seats either side facing each other two by two. Well, not that she could say she was alone, she mentally qualified. This compartment looked to be full, with about fifty fellow travellers, she thought, all Westerners by the look. So apart from the list of names and addresses she had been given of the people on her tour, that must mean there was more than one tour heading in the same direction.

'Hello.' She turned her head to see that a pretty mousy-haired girl had appeared from somewhere behind her and was sporting the same badge that had been supplied to her to identify her as being with the 'China Expedition' group. 'I'm Betsy Warren,' the friendly girl told her, her Australian accent starting to come through. 'You must be

Lauretta Frost. I've checked everybody else out from the list they gave us.'

'Hello,' Laurie said, about to invite the other girl to call her Laurie. But Betsy was showing herself to be a talkative person and was going on:

'I'm travelling with my sister Shirley. Isn't this great! We only finished a Japan tour yesterday . . . .'

She broke off as the coach attendant came to where Laurie was sitting carrying the largest kettle she had ever seen, and asking, by pointing to the large china cup complete with lid sitting on the shelf-like table, if she wanted tea.

'Please,' said Laurie, watching avidly as hot water was poured on top of the jasmine tea leaves reposing in the bottom.

'I'd better get back,' said Betsy. 'See you later, Lauretta.'

Cheered and feeling less alone for having Betsy come and talk to her, Laurie looked up from her steaming tea. And it was then she met full on the staring look of a dark-haired man she had noticed in the compartment earlier. He hadn't been looking at her before, but he was in no hurry to take his eyes from her now, she saw.

Laurie dropped her eyes to study her cup, not knowing why the intent regard of the man should bother her. Or perhaps she did, she thought a moment later, trying to get to grips with her feeling of being suspicious of everybody who had looked at her a second longer than necessary, when it had never bothered her before. It was that wretched ring again. She had had to bring it with her; there had been nothing else for it.

Certain as she had been that someone had been in her flat, it had been unthinkable to leave it behind. Maurice would go up the wall if she had to tell him it had been stolen. But keeping it in her possession wherever she went was a bother she could do without. Not that she remembered she had it with her all the time.

But there had been moments when her imagination had gone wild and she could have sworn she was being followed. Oh, she had been able to laugh at her imaginings afterwards, but remembering particularly that afternoon she had visited the Museum of History, housed in one room on the fourth floor of a large building in Kowloon, she had been sure then the only other visitor looking at the exhibits had been following her. It had made her wary of going out alone when darkness fell. But that wasn't so much of a chore, since it gave her the opportunity to write long newsy letters home to her parents, to her brother James at university, and also to Kay.

Laurie forgot about the man who had been, if not watching her, then at least making a special note of her existence, as the train travelled on. Her attention being taken with the scene viewed from the window—flat, yellowish-brown fields, trees of sage green, small villages, shanty type buildings, some buildings quaintly attractive. She was unaware of anything in the compartment as she looked out as telegraph poles whizzed by, seeing how immaculately set out and furrowed all the fields they passed seemed to be. The small neat allotments of land, workers at their labours carrying what looked like heavy loads across their shoulders, were of much greater interest to her.

Her attention was pulled back to the compartment as the navy blue uniformed attendant began wet-mopping the aisle as they sped along. Damn, her eyes had had to go in *his* direction again! She looked away, having noted that he wasn't wearing a tour badge of any kind on that expensive-looking sweater. So, unlike her, he must have every confidence of finding his way about, even in China. He had that look about him, she thought, as though he would always know precisely where he was, exactly what he was doing.

She forgot about him again as the train began to slow down. People began to stir, get their belongings together. She had last seen her suitcase at the railway station, but had her thick padded coat ready to put on the moment they reached Peking, as it was said to be fourteen degrees centigrade below freezing up there.

The train stopped, and clutching her handbag and camera, her thick coat over her arm, Laurie trooped out of the train glad to see the guide from China Expedition Tours was waiting for them.

And it was in the car park of Canton railway station that the members of the group she was to travel with sorted themselves out—the man in the train was not one of them.

'We will tour the city,' the guide informed them as they filled up the seats in the small bus. 'Then dinner, then to the airport, then you will fly to Peking.'

Laurie had a seat to herself on the right of the bus, the double seats on the left being occupied by people who were travelling together. But it didn't upset her that she appeared to be the only one without a companion as she tried to find room for her long legs in the small space the seat in front allowed.

She was too busy as they set off in trying to listen to what the guide was saying in his broken English—all his R's coming out L's while at the same time looking out of the window, seeing her first trolley-bus, and trying to accustom her ears to the constant sound of motor-horns.

They had had a meal at the border where there had been no condescension to Western ways, chopsticks being the order of the day. And it was the same at dinner, though since a mid-fifties couple, Mr and Mrs Dodd, she discovered, had the same non-expertise as her, she didn't feel so much of an idiot when a piece of meat she had successfully held dropped from her chopsticks just before she got it to her mouth.

'We'll be experts when we leave,' the salt-and-pepper-haired Mrs Dodd told her confidently as she witnessed the incident. 'That, or as thin as laths!'

The plane journey to Peking took over two hours, and Laurie was more impressed by the smartness of Peking airport than she had been by the airport at Canton, having yet to learn that spittoons were not an uncommon sight in China still.

The cold air hit them when they came from the airport to their bus. 'I don't care what it looks like,' exclaimed Mrs Dodd, having a sense of humour Laurie took to, 'but this hat is going on my head and staying there until we get somewhere warm!' She then proceeded to put on a large woolly hat, pulling it well down over her ears, and looked so like Laurie's idea of a Tartar of old, she just had to grin.

'It looks great,' she told her, feeling snug in her own white woolly hat her mother had knitted her but which she had never thought she would wear, although it had a certain chic to it.

It was quite late when they arrived at their hotel, but it was such a thrill to actually be there, actually in Peking, that when she was issued with her key to a room on the second floor, Laurie had to remember that the guide had declared an early start tomorrow, so she had better get to bed as soon as possible.

Her room seemed vast after the smallness of the accommodation in Mei Lai's flat. And she was surprised to see she had a T.V. in her room, plus a hot water flask, a cup complete with lid, and a canister of tea. But with the early start scheduled for the next morning in mind, she investigated only to see that the central heating pipes beneath the window were hot, and that she had her own bathroom, then a quick wash and she went out like a light.

The next morning, knowing it was going to be perishing

cold outside, she donned a thick pair of knitted tights under her jeans, and added an extra sweater. Then remembering that the guide had said they could change travellers cheques in the lobby, Chinese currency being unobtainable outside the country, she took her Hong Kong wallet with her remaining ten Hong Kong dollars and small supply of travellers cheques in it from the bottom of her suitcase and left her room, handing in her key to the man on duty at the desk on her floor.

Breakfast was a satisfying meal, more so because she had a knife and fork. How otherwise she would have managed the bacon and eggs served, she shuddered to think. Not lingering with the others who had arrived late having gone to get their currency first, she went out into the foyer and up to the desk where money was being exchanged.

And it was there that she saw *him* again—the man in the train. He came and stood by her while she waited her turn. He was tall, she noted, his eyes dark brown, she saw at close quarters, his nose straight, chin square with an iron determined look to it. His physique was one many a man would have envied, she couldn't help thinking, seeing he looked to have muscle power without being musclebound.

Having decided it was ridiculous to think everyone she came into contact with was after Anona's ring, Laurie still couldn't help the feeling that there was something faintly sinister about him. He could have looked away from her first in the train yesterday, but he hadn't, she remembered, as studiously she tried to pretend she had missed seeing his lofty height.

Then she had to be glad he was there. She found out he was as English as she was when her lack of being a world traveller showed itself in the way she couldn't understand the Chinese girl when she handed back the travellers cheque she had given her.

'Sign it at the bottom,' he told her in even unregional-accented tones.

'Oh yes,' she said, having forgotten the bank had told her she had to do that when she had already signed her cheques at the top in front of the English bank clerk.

The thirty pounds she was exchanging seemed a paltry sum as she waited for her money, in view of the hundred-pound cheque he had in his hand. But by the look of him, he had had no need to watch his spending the past six months like she had, or to clear out his bank account to afford the trip.

She saw him again in Tian'anmen Square, the square where Chairman Mao had in 1949 proclaimed the founding of the People's Republic of China. She had been happily clicking away with her inexpensive camera at the Great Hall of the People, and was backing away trying to get a long shot of the vast square that could hold half a million people, when she saw him. He had seen her, too, she thought, although he had turned away when she had spotted him. He was wearing a sheepskin coat, and like every other man around was wearing a hat, his suiting him particularly in the shape of astrakhan fur.

So he *was* on a tour, she mused, intending to take her long shot whether he was about or not. He seemed to be with a group that had been at a table near hers at break-fast time. She tried to concentrate on the picture she wanted to take, knowing her camera just wasn't up to the shot she wanted, but snapping what she could of the square anyway while wondering what it was about him that disturbed her so. It wasn't as if she was afraid of men or anything like that. Aside from the various boy-friends she had had since she was sixteen, she got on well and easily with Maurice and the men in the lab. Was it all on account of that ring that she was wary? she had to wonder.

'Mr Chan is signalling for us to go.' Betsy Warren came

up to her, her footsteps going in the direction of the bus. Laurie fell into step with her. 'I got a terrific photo of the Monument to the People's Heroes—did you know it's one hundred and twenty four feet high?' Betsy chatted away, her voice carrying, in no way subdued that they were nearing that sheepskin-clad figure. 'Hi,' she even called to him. 'We're off to the Summer Palace—probably see you there.'

'Do you know him?' Laurie questioned when they were far enough away for Betsy's reply not to be overheard.

'No, but I'd certainly like to. He's got the lot, hasn't he?' Then seeing an American young man in his early twenties who was travelling with his father on their tour, 'Though that Mervyn isn't bad, if my luck's out.' And, not waiting for Laurie's comment, 'Poor old Shirl reckoned she was going down with frostbite. She went back to the bus ten minutes ago.'

It was at the Summer Palace, which Laurie learned was also known as the Garden of Harmonious Unity, that she got her first sight of ancient Chinese architecture. Everything was in red, gold, yellow and green, fluted, ridge-tiled buildings and white marble stairs. And it was here that she started to get to know the other members of her tour group as they followed their guide through the many halls, passing comment with each other on the objects of jade, ivory and pearl decorating most of the halls they stayed to look at. All of them stopped when Mr Chan had something to tell them, finding that with the many Chinese who had come to view their own inheritance, when they grouped round to listen to their guide, so too did the Chinese crowd round—though not to listen to Mr Chan, but to look with gentle curiosity at the Westerners.

They were just leaving the Hall of Happiness where the far from benevolent Empress Dowager Ci Xi had lived, when Laurie again felt the sensation that someone was watching her. Unable to repress the instinct, she swung round and found she was right. For the man Betsy had called 'Hi' to, and told him where they were going, was there. And it was as clear as day that he had no interest in the exhibits, for his eyes were fastened on her, his look neither smiling nor friendly.

Laurie didn't smile either as she turned smartly about and hurried after the others—ever present in her mind that she mustn't lose sight of them and get herself lost. There had been none of his tour with him, she thought, as she caught up with her party. Nor had they passed them. So that must mean he had come on in front of his group—or that he had come without them. Now why would he do that? Was he following her?

Don't be ridiculous, Laurie, she counselled herself, wondering for the umpteenth time why she had let Maurice talk her into looking after that ring. That man was an individualist, it stuck out a mile. The others might be content to troop around with a tour, she was quite happy to do so herself, but he looked to be a man who would always go his own way. And the fact that he had been looking at her didn't mean a thing other than as the only other Westerner in the Hall of Happiness when he had got there, she must have stuck out like a sore thumb. It was natural that his eyes would be drawn to her.

She was still wondering why, if he didn't intend to stay with his tour, he had joined a tour in the first place, when Burt, Mervyn's father, came up to her complaining it would take a week to see just this palace alone, yet they were supposed to do it all in a couple of hours.

'Not very long, is it?' she agreed, her camera having been busy as she had tried to record as much of it as she could. 'Still, it's better than not coming at all, isn't it?'

Burt seemed to gravitate to her for the rest of the morning. Whenever they stopped he seemed to be close by. And as she felt in no way threatened by him, seeing that since Mervyn seemed to be doing his best to separate the two sisters, Betsy and Shirley, and that rather left Burt on his own, it was natural, since he appeared to need someone, that he should seek the company of the only other person without a companion.

She could have done with him or anyone that afternoon when they paid a visit to the Temple of Azure Clouds. For somehow or other she had got herself separated from the others, and knew that sensation of being lost of old. The trouble was, in England she could ask just anybody and they would put her right, but this was China, where the chance of her making herself understood if she asked anyone the way back to the bus was remote.

As she tried not to panic, her feeling of being lost was added to as that familiar feeling of being followed assailed her, though this time she would have welcomed it had her pursuer been the man in the sheepskin coat. He at least did speak English. She had just climbed some steps and was about to go through a red and gold dagoba when she turned. There was no one there. Her feeling of being followed had played her false. Yet it was still there when she went where she thought the rest of her group had gone, up another flight of steps, through another dagoba. She turned, about to look through the archway, then caught a flash of red to her right. Betsy was wearing a red coat. Promptly, forgetting her feeling of being followed, Laurie chased after her, just in time to see her disappearing into one of the buildings. Laurie followed.

When she entered the building she at first thought it was nothing more than a badly lit store room. And then as she stared about her, and all thought of Betsy went from her mind, fascination set in as she saw that the store the room held was row upon row of statues of gold-painted disciples of Buddha. Her attention riveted, she walked up and down the several gangways, staring, lost to the world, at the various expressions on what must be five hundred or more statues, some in various stages of decay.

And then suddenly she had bumped into something solid. Her head shot up as two hands came out to steady her, her eyes widening in recognition.

'You'll get yourself lost if you don't look where you're going,' said that same voice that had told her where to sign her travellers cheque that morning.

'What are you doing here?' she challenged, unnerved at seeing him there.

'The same as you, I imagine,' he retorted coolly.

Suddenly she was overwhelmingly conscious of his hands still on her arms. 'Well, I'm not likely to fall over if you let go of me,' she said ungraciously, pointedly—and heard that he could be pretty acid too when he chose.

'My intention was to stop you before you attempted to walk through me, not to rape you,' he told her bluntly, letting go her arms.

Knowing she owed him an apology for her rudeness, she didn't like that he in turn had been equally rude. She spotted Betsy out of the corner of her eye. 'Well, bully for you,' she retorted, no apology forthcoming as she sidestepped him and charged after her.

After that small experience of getting separated from her party, Laurie made up her mind to keep in close contact with them as she wrapped up warmly the next morning, already enthusiastic about the proposed half day trip to the Great Wall of China.

By now everyone in her group had sorted themselves and knew each other by name. But it still came as something of a surprise that Betsy should know not only the names of everyone on their tour, but also at least one name on the tour that seemed to be coinciding with theirs. Perhaps it shouldn't have surprised her, Laurie thought, for Betsy was a gregarious creature. They were in the train heading for the best preserved section of the Wall, at Badaling, when the young Australian girl came and plonked herself down beside her, camera round her neck, saying:

'If I go on taking photographs at this rate,' pausing as she snapped a three horse drawn cart through the train window, 'I shall have more film than clothes to take back to Perth!' She checked her camera, making sure it was ready for her next shot, then remarked, 'Have you noticed Tyler is the only one of all of us who isn't toting a camera?'

'Tyler?' Laurie queried, not knowing a face in their party who fitted the name.

'That dishy guy on the other trip—don't say you don't know who I mean? He's the only one of that crowd that any girl would leave home for.'

Laurie had no trouble in knowing whom Betsy was talking about. She had been hoping he wouldn't be anywhere around today in view of their short sharp exchange yesterday. She was on holiday and could do without any unpleasantness, and he just seemed to bring out the worst in her.

'Er—you've had a few words with him, then?' she queried, unable to quell her curiosity although she was sure she wasn't that interested.

'Not yet,' said Betsy blithely. 'But the day is yet young,' explaining, 'I overheard one of his group calling him Tyler.'

Betsy's remark about the day being yet young gave Laurie the ominous impression that he was around somewhere and that Betsy was hoping to get into conversation with him before they returned to the hotel. Yet she hadn't seen him board the train.

'I haven't seen him today,' she said carefully, to which Betsy gave her a look that said how could she ever have missed seeing him, before she recalled:

'Our bus arrived at the station before his, but he's here all right. Sitting at the back.'

'Well, good hunting,' said Laurie while at the same time wondering why she should suddenly feel uptight. After her rudeness yesterday he was more likely to cut her than bother to come up to speak to her. She thought a change of conversation was needed. 'I thought you were getting on well with Mervyn, though?'

Her ploy worked, as instantly Betsy forgot the man she fancied above all others, and grimaced comically as she said, 'Would you believe it wasn't me the rat was after, but our Shirl? Still, it makes her happy and takes her mind off her frostbite.' And as suddenly as she had come, Betsy was off again. 'I'll go and have a chat to Burt,' she said over her shoulder.

Cold wasn't the word for it as under their guide's instructions they all piled out of the train and all tourist parties mixed together, getting on any of the several buses that were to take them the short distance to the Wall.

Laurie had no trouble seeing the man she now knew as Tyler, but she studiously avoided seeing him. Avoided seeing him too when at their destination they disembarked and listened to the guide instructing them that they should return at twelve to take a bus back to the train. Then, turning to the awesome construction said to be the only man-made structure visible to the naked eye from the moon, he told them that they could take the east or the west paths, but that the east part was easier.

'Let's go west!' exclaimed Mrs Dodd. And in view of her and her husband being the more senior of the group, rather than lose face and take the easier route, all of them followed.

All of them, that was, but Laurie, and she hung back. She was sure she wasn't getting paranoic about *him*, Tyler, but some basic instinct she had never known she possessed was telling her to avoid him, telling her when she saw his party move off following her group, that since he was such a perfectly fit-looking specimen, he too would take the west route.

She fought a silent inner battle as she remembered her thoughts that morning that she was going to stick like glue to the others, and so eliminate any chance of getting lost. She studied the wall for another few seconds, saw it went straight up so therefore must come straight down, and decided on that instant that she couldn't possibly get lost—then she moved east.

She then forgot all about him. Awe, wonder was setting in. Again that marvellous feeling of actually being there, actually standing on part of a construction it had taken three hundred thousand men ten years to join together the several walls built by independent kingdoms. She was actually standing there on the wall that stretched for nearly four thousand miles.

It took some time to sink in as, busy with her camera, she took snap after snap, pausing to click into place another cartridge of film as she photographed the parapet, the towers, the rugged dark hills and ridges. There was not a blade of grass to be seen anywhere, making it seem impossible that in summer those black-brown hills would be covered in greenery. It was so cold one had to keep moving, yet in summer people would walk the wall in shirt sleeves.

Time and again she walked, getting steadily warmer, for the wall wound upwards, causing her to wonder how the others were doing on the west climb. Once she was stopped by Chinese peasants trying to get her to part with her yuan in exchange for old coins or a tiny silver Buddha which were said to have been taken from the burial places of the dead. The idea appalled her. 'No, thank you,' she repeated many times.

Yet she was loving every minute of the experience. The spirit of adventure soared in her blood when, going through an archway, she saw some steps leading up to a tower. Her padded coat was cumbersome, so she roped her camera around her neck, needing a hand on either rail as she climbed the stone steps to the lookout.

She soon felt quite warm, so the bitterly cold wind that greeted her was a shock, took her breath and had her going to the far wall for shelter. But she was glad she had made the effort. She was careless of the wind and grateful for her white woolly hat, as she had a better view of the parapet walk, ahead on top of the hill the tower she was aiming to make for.

The cold was getting through to her, so she turned, intending to go down again, and saw then that she was not the only one who had decided to climb that particular tower.

'I thought you'd gone with the others!' left her before she could hold it back.

'So you did notice me, for all you were pretending not to,' Tyler remarked, his voice mocking so that her feelings to him at that moment were fairly violent, especially since her blurted out exclamation had left her without a leg to stand on.

'If you've gathered that much, you must also have gathered that it's my wish to avoid seeing you,' she retorted at last, not seeing any reason to wrap up the fact that she didn't care much for him.

'Why should you wish to avoid me?' he asked, being deliberately obtuse, she thought. 'You were rude to me yesterday entirely without cause when all I did was to hang on to you to save you from hurting yourself.'

She didn't feel like apologising. Which again was unlike her, endorsing for her that this man brought out the worst in her. She walked by him, heading for the steps to go down.

'Are you afraid of me?'

His voice came silkily, close by, so he must be right

behind her. 'Why should I be afraid?' she turned to challenge him—then found she was looking into dark brown eyes, felt her heart miss a beat, and for some unknown reason, wanted to run.

'You tell me,' he challenged right back.

She couldn't tell him because she didn't know. 'Oh, leave me alone!' she snapped. Which was no answer at all, but was all she could manage before she turned and needed all her concentration to go down the steps.

She couldn't hear him behind her as she carried on walking up the incline towards the topmost tower she had seen. But she was sure he was there. And she began to dislike him even more that because of his suspected presence, she couldn't turn round as she wanted to and take in the view of the way she had come.

And she wasn't afraid of him anyway. She had reasoned last night that no one was after that wretched ring. The only reason she had thought they might be, she had seen clearly then, was because she felt weighted down with the responsibility of it.

But she blamed him that this visit to the Great Wall, the highlight of the tour, had been spoilt because he was trailing her footsteps. Yet if she wasn't afraid of him—and she was sure she wasn't—and if he was not after the ring, which again she was sure he wasn't, what was it about him that had made her feel so antagonistic towards him from that first moment she had caught him watching her?

She had been walking steadily towards the tower she had set her sights on reaching, when she abandoned the idea of investigating it.

It was all his fault, she thought, halting her steps. She didn't want another encounter with him when she got there. She turned, the idea in her mind of ignoring him, of walking past him and going to the café she had seen signposted close to the Wall for a cup of coffee.

Since she was certain he was right behind her, it was a

shock to see that though there were several Westerners mixed in with the Chinese coming towards her—a babble of French hit her ears as several French people passed— the man Tyler wasn't among them.

She wasn't piqued that he wasn't following her, for goodness' sake, she thought, quashing the very idea that the emotion that hit her might be disappointment. But as she had turned about, feeling hot after her climb, the idea of coffee that had been born still seemed a very good idea.

Then she took a wrong turn and had to retrace her steps before she found that the café, a large room with big round tables plus a part of it that sold souvenirs, was no more than she was used to. There were not many people there, so she had her pick of the tables, though first she took off her thick coat and draped it over a chair. She had just sat down, a hand to the hat on her head, when someone coming in through the door attracted her attention.

Her hand stayed in its action when Tyler came straight to her table—just as though he knew she was there, though from the wide expanse of glass fronting the café, he could well have seen her from the window, and as casually as you like he sat down in the chair next to her.

She still hadn't found her voice at his colossal impudence, though she had pulled her hat from her head and made some attempt to fluff her hair out when he remarked admiringly:

'That's right. It's a pity to keep such gloriously coloured hair covered up. Tell me, do you have the temper that usually goes with the beautiful red hair you possess?'

Impudence wasn't the word! she thought, her lips firming. And yes, there had been occasions in her formative years when her temper had been positively volcanic. But that had been before she had learned to count ten before exploding.

'I usually manage to keep it under control,' she told him tightly.

'Good,' he said, not a bit abashed. 'Have you ordered yet?'

'I've only just arrived,' she told him shortly, wondering why she had the feeling he knew that already, before it came to her since he had probably seen her shedding her coat through the window the conclusion was obvious.

She had to admire him even though her spirit of independence had her wanting to order her own coffee, to hear him summon the waiter and order coffee for both of them in Mandarin.

'Did you want anything to eat?' he thought to ask, then dismissed the waiter at Laurie's tight-lipped shake of her head. He gave her cause to admire him some more when he shed his sheepskin, revealing a broad width of shoulder that had nothing to do with the padding of numerous sweaters that almost everyone was clad in.

Alarmed at the direction her thoughts were taking, averting her eyes from his firm mouth with the lower lip that suggested his kisses might be quite something, Laurie was horrified that she might be a quick second member of the fan club Betsy had instigated. Good grief, she didn't even like the man!

'So tell me,' Tyler enquired, settling himself down, 'what's a nice girl like you doing in a place like this?'

CHAPTER THREE

THAT his remark had her lips wanting to twitch, Laurie did not want to allow. 'The same as you, I imagine,' she replied, using the same expression he had used yesterday. 'Though on second thoughts, where's your camera? Or,' as a sudden thought came to her, 'have you been here before?'

Their coffee was brought to them, but not the bill, which since she was determined to pay for her own she would like to have caught sight of.

'Have you?' she asked when the waiter went away and Tyler hadn't answered.

'I have, actually,' he admitted, his eyes scrutinising her. 'But it's well worth a second visit, wouldn't you agree?'

She had to, of course. She had barely seen enough this time, and she felt cross about that since it was unlikely she would ever come this way again. But there was no time now to hurry out of the café and make for that tower once more.

'You speak Mandarin, I noticed,' she said, since they were being fairly amicable now, and she did not want to have another battle of words. She would be gone anyway as soon as she had finished her coffee, and she really would stick close to the others in future.

'Only a smattering,' he disclaimed. Then he was asking, 'What made you decide to come on holiday on your own?'

Laurie could easily have asked him the same question. About to say, 'I enjoy my own company,' she bit down the barb. He would know it for the pointed remark it was anyway, since she was on a tour with a dozen other

43

people, though why she should worry about his feelings she hadn't a clue.

'I wasn't going to come alone,' she found herself saying honestly instead. 'Only at the last moment my . . .' she paused, thinking with his air of sophistication he would be bored to tears if she went into details about Kay's appendicitis, '. . . my friend couldn't make it.'

And then she was sorely tempted to forget all about counting up to ten, when his look hardened and he grunted, 'His wife put the block on, did she?'

'Why, you . . .!' she began, before self-control won.

Still fuming, she tried to catch the eye of the waiter, and felt more angry than ever that all her signals were ignored. Damn him, let him pay the bill! she thought furiously, knowing she had been right to dislike Tyler whatever-his-name-was on sight.

She stood up, had her coat on and was at the door of the café pulling on her white hat, before she had thought further. She had left him sitting there and hoped they overcharged him.

But outside her temper rapidly cooled—though it had little to do with the below freezing temperature that hit her. It was all very well storming out in high dudgeon that the man in there thought so lightly of her morals that he thought it was not beyond her to have an affair with a married man. But having so hastily left him, she hadn't a clue which way to go to catch the bus to the train. And what was worse, there was not another Western-looking person about at that precise moment whom she could ask.

Well, she wasn't going back in to enquire, that was for sure, she thought, moving away from the café window.

Of course it didn't help matters at all that she had taken a path that led nowhere near where she thought she should be. Nor did it make her feel any better that Tyler had come after her. Not that he appeared to recognise that she was lost.

'I think you must have photographed everything in sight,' he said, handing her the camera she had left behind in her rush, 'but you might need that if anything else takes your fancy.'

'Thank you,' she muttered, taking it from him.

'Seen enough?' he enquired.

Of you, she wanted to retort. 'Yes,' she said quietly.

'Then if you have no strong objection I'll walk to the bus with you.'

How could she object? She needed him. Then she found, as he took hold of her arm and turned her about, that he wasn't waiting for any objection she might have. 'We'll go this way, shall we,' he stated rather than asked, letting go her arm as she fell into step with him.

Feeling better that someone else was doing the navigating, like a lamb Laurie trotted beside him, though nowhere near to forgetting his remark she considered totally uncalled for.

He didn't appear to have anything he wanted to say to her either, as slowing down his long stride to match hers, silently he walked along.

Hoping that when they did reach the bus she would find a seat to herself, Laurie went with him down an incline. She found they were soon in the area where she had separated from Mr Chan and the others, but she still wasn't too sure of her bearings till they turned a corner, still going downwards, where she saw a sign pointing to the railway station.

Having come this far with Tyler she couldn't very well now leave him, she considered. Especially since he was going in the same direction and she would either have to run on in front to part from him or dawdle behind.

Her thoughts shut off abruptly as they turned another corner and a wind so fierce hit them it had her gasping for breath, grateful for the hand that gripped her arm as her legs were threatened to be swept from under her.

Bracing herself against the wind, she heard Tyler say a few short sharp words in Mandarin to the peasants who had braved the cold and wind to try and sell their macabre burial trinkets. Then as she spotted a couple of buses not far away, another blast of wind blew up, gathering a dust storm in the process, and she was blinded by what felt like an eye full of road.

Eyes tightly closed, she clutched at Tyler. 'My eye,' she said above the wind. 'I've got something in my eye,' then felt relief from the windy blast as he came and stood firmly in front of her.

'I can't do a thing about it if you don't open your eyes,' came his voice calmly. 'Which one is it?'

'The right one,' she told him, both eyes watering. Vanity, for all her distress, made her glad she had decided against putting mascara on her already dark long lashes that morning.

Tyler's ungloved hand felt warm on her cheek, causing a peculiar feeling to start up inside her at the feel of that warm hand as he turned her head in the direction he wanted it.

He had to instruct her again to open her eyes as with a large white handkerchief in his other hand he found and cleared away the alien matter. Her right eye watering more than the other one when he had finished, Laurie blinked rapidly several times—then stopped blinking as gently he mopped up the tear that had run down her cheek, wiped dry both eyes with that same gentleness, so that her vision returned to normal at last. Laurie stood and stared at him, trying to equate his gentle touch with the aggressive side she had seen in him.

He was unmoving too, making no attempt to turn and go on their way as the wind buffeted him. He stood looking down at her, his eyes narrowed as though trying to read from her eyes what went on inside of her. Then suddenly his head was coming nearer.

'This is because I offended you back at the café,' he said, bending his head to lightly kiss her mouth, his apology, if it was such, being delivered with such charm she hadn't the wit to draw back. 'And this,' he said, as though he liked the feel of her mouth against his and kissing her lightly once more, 'is to kiss it better.'

The odd sensations his light kisses aroused, memory stirring that she had thought his kisses would be quite something, had a battle warring inside Laurie that she was hopeful he knew nothing about.

'Thank you for attending to my eye,' she said primly, trying frantically to remember she didn't even like him, telling herself his apology for his remark still didn't negate that he had said such a thing, 'but you can keep your kisses for those that want them!' And regardless that the head wind would stop her from charging in front of him, she brushed past him, keeping her head down as she made for the transport and shelter.

She knew he was right beside her, but determinedly pretended she didn't. She reached the first bus and was aboard, taking a seat next to an Indian-looking gentleman so that Tyler would know she had no intention of sitting with him.

Gradually the bus filled up, Orientals and Westerners getting inside as quickly as they could away from the biting wind. But none, Laurie saw, from her tour or Tyler's.

When the time came and the bus set off for its short run to the station, Laurie was still no nearer to understanding the odd feelings he had aroused in her when his hand had touched her cheek, his lips had touched hers. She'd been kissed before, for goodness' sake, but never had she felt that same—awareness?

Oh, bother the man! she thought. She didn't like him and that was all there was to it. That her body chemistry was playing some little game of its own had nothing to do with that basic fact.

Everyone disembarked at the terminus. And as Laurie got out too she checked her watch and saw there was still some time to go before she met up with her group.

She pulled her woolly hat farther down as the cold got to her, looking around hoping to see someone she knew, except *him*. But everyone seemed to be in pairs or groups huddled together chatting, no shelter around that she could see apart from a brick built building across the road.

She crossed the road to the building. At least if she stood round the side of that wall she would be out of the wind. It was a good vantage point too to watch for the next bus to come down that hill. Perhaps her group would be on the next one.

As she settled herself against the wall, a voice came that she was beginning to know all too well.

'You'll freeze if you don't keep moving.'

She looked up and saw she had company, everyone else obviously had found shelter elsewhere. And it seemed to her then that there was only her and Tyler in that whole barren spot.

'Come on,' he coaxed, a hint of that same charm he had used earlier. 'Stop looking mulish. Come and behave like a tourist.'

'Tourist?' she questioned, not seeing anything wrong in being a tourist, not meaning to speak to him either—but too late now.

'You haven't run out of film, have you?'

Was he being sarcastic? She thought he was, and didn't care much that he appeared to be dissociating himself from anything as lowly as a tourist, or the fact he had witnessed she was camera happy.

A hot retort rose to her lips. She quelled it—just. The idea came to her that since her sour tongue didn't seem to have the effect of making him leave her alone, she would try boring him out of his skull instead.

'Actually I have plenty of film with me,' she said, just as though she was taking his remark at face value. 'I bought loads and loads of it in Hong Kong. Now what was the name of the place?—not that it's important. I know where it is if I need to buy more when I get back.' His face was impassive, but she hadn't done yet. 'Though I shall have to change some travellers cheques first, I'm down to my last ten Hong Kong dollars. But that. . . .' she broke off. A light of interest had come to Tyler's eyes.

Was it interest, though? Or was it that her prattle, her attempt to shake him off had amused him? Whatever it was, it left her feeling a fool that she had ever bothered to try. Her tongue froze along with the rest of her.

'You're standing here waiting to meet someone?' he queried, ignoring what she had just said by suggesting that since she hadn't moved from the spot, there must be some good reason.

'I'm waiting for my tour group,' she replied snappily, ready to fire up if he made so much as half a crack intimiating that she wasn't choosey who she had an affair with, whether they be single or married.

'They won't be here for another fifteen minutes,' he told her, arrogantly knowledgeable. And, his voice going on to being teasing, 'If you haven't worn out your camera clicking finger why not take a photo of that camel?'

'What camel?' she asked, forgetting to be mad at him.

'Down there.'

Laurie looked where he was indicating, and saw that down below a patch of rough ground, fenced in by a double-barred wooden structure, was a two-humped camel she hadn't spotted.

It was the cold as much as anything that had her going with him, she decided, as gingerly she stepped over frozen patches of ice, over rough terrain, keeping her distance, not wanting his help in any way.

But it was well worth the constant threat of going base over apex and landing in a heap when she got there. And regardless of his teasing, she focussed her camera, lowering it down from a pale blue sky and getting the sun to her back. It was a good picture she thought, before she brought the shutter down. There was even a line of green in the background, the first greenery she had seen in this past couple of hours. Click, and she had it.

Tyler was being very indulgent, she thought, when he said, 'Give me your camera, I'll take one of you with the camel in the background.'

'My mother would like that,' she said, forgetting she didn't like him as she handed her camera over.

'Smile,' he instructed, and when feeling stupid standing there while he aligned the picture she kept her face immobile. But try as she might, the smile wouldn't come. 'Say Caerphilly,' he said. She grinned, and heard the click.

'Idiot,' she said, taking her camera back. And, thinking she was being too friendly, 'I'm going back to see if the others have arrived.'

If she'd taken it more slowly, if he hadn't smiled, unoffended that she had called him an idiot, if that smile hadn't affected her so that she had felt the need to hurry away from him, then she would have seen she was going to come to grief as her legs went north and south like some newborn colt. But when she was sure she was going to hit the hard ground with a thump, two firm arms came hard around her. And it was instinct alone that had her forgetting her enmity and hanging on to him while she scrabbled to get her balance.

It took only a few seconds, but his arms were still around her when she discovered the sky was still above, the ground still beneath her feet, that her legs were holding her.

'Thanks,' she tossed at him. She saw his head was

coming nearer, but had already played that game. 'No need to kiss me better,' she said, pulling out of his arms. 'I didn't hurt myself.'

His arms dropped to his sides as he sighed exaggeratedly. 'I'll save it for another time,' he promised.

'You'll be lucky,' she retorted, and turned away, having the good fortune to see Betsy at that particular moment.

More careful now, unable to pretend her ridiculous chemistry hadn't started acting up again to have Tyler's arms around her, Laurie picked her way over the uneven ground, only to find when she rounded the wall of the brick-built building that Betsy had disappeared.

Nonplussed, because there was no one else in sight either, she stood wondering where everyone had gone. A hand grasped her elbow to guide her across the road to what looked like a large temporary workmen's building, and she knew she wasn't completely alone.

Unspeaking, but allowing him to take her across the road purely because he might have some idea of where everyone was, Laurie allowed herself to be escorted. But when they stopped at the workmen's hut, she discovered just by lifting her eyes to the sign above the door, written in English so she could understand it, that it wasn't a workmen's hut at all.

'Foreign Visitors' Waiting Room,' the sign said.

Laurie shrugged off his hold and turned to him, forgetting to count ten. 'You knew damn well it was here all the time!' she snapped.

'Would I have deprived you of taking your first picture of a camel?' he replied, only admiration in evidence as he looked into her green eyes and saw the sparks there, otherwise entirely unmoved by her flash of temper.

Without another word Laurie spun round, needing to get through that door before she obeyed the need to hit him.

Her eyes searched and found Betsy, and she went over,

knowing Tyler had not followed when Betsy greeted only her. 'Come and get warm,' she said. 'Hang on, I'll get you a cup of tea. Though by the flush in your cheeks, you look more hot than cold.'

Luckily the Australian girl didn't seem to be expecting a reply. And as the heat of anger left Laurie, so did the two spots of colour in her cheeks.

'Where are the others?' she asked, when Betsy handed her her tea, not wanting a discussion on her complexion.

'Lazy lot,' Betsy said cheerfully, 'They're all waiting for the bus. I walked down.'

Laurie was glad of her own company on the train journey back. Tyler was in the compartment somewhere, but thank goodness she couldn't see him. She had come near to hitting him back there, she mused, while she wondered what it was about him that had so loosened her temper, years of learning to keep it under control had quickly been forgotten. And who was he to look down on tourists, just as though he wasn't one himself? That sent her down the road of fantasy; of wondering if he were a spy. He spoke Mandarin, didn't he, for all he modestly claimed it was only a smattering.

She brought herself up sharply. Spies were insignificant little men, she was sure of it. And Tyler was neither small or insignificant, he would be noticed wherever he went, even without his height, his whole bearing spoke of a man no one would overlook.

But she just couldn't shake off the thought that he wasn't just a tourist, that he had some other reason for being in China than that of seeing the same sights as the rest of them. He had admitted anyway, hadn't he, that this wasn't his first visit? Perhaps that was why he seemed to look down on tourists—he had done it all before and wasn't seeing it through their new eyes. Perhaps he wasn't even looking down on the rest of them at all, she found herself thinking. Perhaps it just seemed that way to her because she was desperately looking for things not to like in him. Now why should she want to do that?

Some inner self stopped her going down that path in her wonderings. Blow him, she'd missed enough of the scenery, her eyes seeing yet not seeing anything from the window, as her thoughts had gone on.

She concentrated on the view, and saw magnificent ragged ranges, silent and indomitable. She saw tall trees on a still, barren landscape, was aware of the train going slowly round tortuous mountain bends. Unbelieving, she saw sheep high on a hillside and couldn't help but wonder what they fed on.

Music came from a loudspeaker somewhere in the train. Someone singing pleasantly in Chinese began to relax her, making her only just then realise that just thinking of Tyler had made her tense.

That afternoon they toured the Forbidden City, the former Imperial Palace. But on seeing Tyler's tour was right behind them, Laurie didn't allow anything to attract her attention so much that she got left by her group, ever conscious as she was that she could find herself mingling with him and his group if she didn't watch it. As it was she had cut it fine when she'd just had to linger for a last look at the fearsome pair of bronze cast lions that guarded the Gate of Supreme Harmony.

Mrs Dodd echoed the words Burt had said to her when, not having encountered Tyler at all that afternoon though she caught his eyes on her one time, they returned to their hotel.

'I could do with sixty days, not six! I swear we'd only just stepped into the Hall of Supreme Harmony when Mr Chan was ushering us into the Hall of Central Harmony, and before I'd got my breath we were off again to the Hall of Preserving Harmony. Quite frankly,' said Mrs Dodd, 'I'm not feeling very harmonious about it at all, Lauretta.'

Laurie laughed, and so did Mrs Dodd. But in bed that night she couldn't say she objected to the speed with which they had viewed the Forbidden City. It was the one time she hadn't wanted to dawdle. The one time she had, apart from seeing the lions, been up there with the guide every time.

She was at breakfast the next morning when, having got into the same habit as everyone else of taking outdoor things down to breakfast to avoid the necessity of going back upstairs when straight after breakfast they went out, she suddenly remembered she had left her camera in her room.

Leaving her coat with Shirley, she raced up to the second landing, saw no one on duty but, undaunted, reached her hand forward to take the key to her room from its cubbyhole. But there was no key to room 226 there.

Thinking the attendant must be giving her room the once-over, she sprinted round the bend, then pulled up short, a frown wrinkling her otherwise smooth skin as she saw that not only was the door of her room open, but that Tyler was just coming from it.

He had not seen her, but was now busy, engaged in conversation with the room attendant, who also stood by her door. She moved forward and saw Tyler look at her, then had to wonder if her eyes had played her false, for without batting an eyelid, succeeding in looking the picture of innocence, he looked away from her as he carried on his conversation with the small Chinese man.

'*Xie, xie*,' he was saying to the smiling Chinese, making her wonder, since that was the only bit of Mandarin she knew, what Tyler was thanking him for.

The floor attendant answered in a flood of Chinese. But she was too worked up to wait while they finished their discussion. 'Were you in my room?' she demanded, not waiting for Tyler to say anything in reply to the man.

'In your room?' He looked as though the very idea amused him, 'What would I be doing in your room—with your lovely self out of it?'

'Cut out the comedy,' she snapped. 'Were you in there just now?'

She saw the amused look leave him as he realised she was serious. He didn't take very kindly to her accusation, it was clear, as he bit back:

'For your information, I happened to be passing your door just as the floor boy here came out.' His voice took on a sarcastic edge she didn't care for. 'I didn't realise I had to have your permission before, in the interest of East–West relations, I stopped to pass the time of day with him.'

Biting her lip that she had just made an idiot of herself, Laurie fled through the door, slamming it soundly shut behind her. Oh God, that man! What was happening to her?

It was obvious now that he had only been standing there talking. He had probably been standing in her doorway rather than go round to the other side of the trolley the man had close by him. If her brain cogs had wakened up with her that morning, she would have instantly remembered that Tyler could speak Mandarin. And since the floor attendant had been smiling, had been friendly with him, it was doubly obvious that Tyler hadn't been in her room.

Why, only last night she had learned when the same Chinese had returned her laundry how totally honest the man was. She had gone to tip him, but he had rejected her tip, horrified. And she had felt then as though she had committed some unpardonable sin by offering the tip in the first place. He certainly wouldn't have been smiling had Tyler been in a room that hadn't been allocated to him, she was sure. He would have had the manager up to their floor double quick, of that she was positive.

Her prayers were answered when she came out of her room clutching her camera. Neither the floor attendant nor Tyler were there. Grateful for the chance to be able to put the incident from her before she saw him again, Laurie joined the others as they were about to go through the revolving door to the outside January air, the order of the day another palace, another temple.

By the time they returned to the hotel, she had put the incident of that morning out of her mind. Though she hadn't lost that eerie feeling she was being followed. She had shrugged the feeling away, determined not to get neurotic about it. Perhaps everybody experienced that self-same feeling when journeying in a foreign land. At least the gods had been kind to her, for not once had she clapped eyes on Tyler.

She was in her room that night, writing a postcard to her brother, when a knock came on her door. And it was when she opened it that Laurie knew her luck in not seeing Tyler had just run out.

He was wearing a dark sweater over dark trousers, one hand high against the door frame, leaning negligently and seeming happy not to say a word as he surveyed her figure, slimmer now that she had dispensed with her layers of warm clothes.

'Well?' she asked sharply, trying to deny how attractive she found him.

A smile tugged at the corner of his mouth. 'Stop pretending you don't like me and come and have a drink with me.'

Cheeky devil! She ignored the first part of his remark; to deny she was pretending would only stress that she felt anything for him at all.

'Thank you—no,' she replied sweetly. And in case he thought she had come down with the last shower, 'I bought a bottle of Moutai too—to take home to my father. A hundred and six proof, I believe the label said.'

'You think I'm inviting you to my room intending to get you popped up with the local firewater?'

'Aren't you?' she challenged, and saw his smile broaden, in no way flattened that she had seen straight through him.

'It would rather defeat the object, wouldn't it,' he said sardonically, 'if in my endeavour to get you to lose what inhibitions you might have, I made you drunk and—er—incapable in the process?'

His not wrapping up what this conversation was all about had warm colour coming to her cheeks. Damn him, why *did* he disturb her so? About to close the door on him without another word, she heard him telling her she had got it all wrong.

'As a matter of fact,' he said before the door had moved more than a few inches, 'even I, since your opinion of me seems to be gutter level, have more subtlety than that. I was asking you to have a drink in the bar downstairs.'

'Bar?' she countered, not ready to believe him. 'This hotel hasn't got a bar.'

'Not a bar as we know one,' he agreed. 'But the dining room is used for that purpose after the evening meal has been cleared away. There were a dozen or more people in there imbibing when I had a look a few minutes ago.'

'Oh,' said Laurie, feeling prickles of embarrassment that she had brought this conversation on herself.

'So you see,' he said loftily, making no allowances for her embarrassment, made obvious by the fact that she found his sweater of interest and wouldn't meet his eyes, 'you had no grounds for your mucky little thoughts.'

That brought her head up sharply. How dared he talk of her having mucky thoughts? His footsteps had seemed to dog hers everywhere she went. He had kissed her and said he would save his next kiss for another time.

'Are you trying to tell me the thought of trying to seduce me has never entered your head?' she challenged, angry enough not to care that she was being as open as him.

'You mean there's a chance?' he mocked.

'No, there damn well isn't!' she blazed, and regardless whether anyone was having an early night or not, she slammed the door shut in his face.

The cheeky swine! she fumed, her fast sprung anger taking much longer to cool. Who the hell did he think he was! Was he so used to women falling for him like ninepins that all he thought he had to do was to crook his little finger and they would tumble into bed with him?

Half an hour later she went to bed, her anger gone, the knowledge with her that yes, a man like that Tyler creature would have women falling all over themselves for him. Well, he needn't think she was going to join that happy band! she thought, thumping her pillow. Though why it should bother her and keep sleep from coming that he -probably had a veritable harem tucked away somewhere, she didn't know.

CHAPTER FOUR

As Laurie had her mind set on ignoring Tyler the next time she saw him, it was frustrating to see him in conversation with several people in the huge foyer the following morning, entirely unaware that she was there. There went her opportunity of showing him for further reference that she was cutting him, she thought, when not so much as a glance did he flick her way before she had to follow her party out to the bus.

That morning they visited a commune. They were invited to take tea and ask any questions they wished of the Director, before they were taken first into one of the dwellings, small but immaculate, where a retired couple lived. Astonished, Laurie couldn't believe her eyes when, in the bedroom, she saw that the bed, on a brick-built base about eighteen inches high, had an aperture where fuel was burned to keep the bed warm. It seemed hazardous to say the least, though maybe with the temperature so raw outside, it was a hazard worth taking.

Next they went to a kindergarten where delightful three-year-olds got up and danced for them, not a little pushing and shoving taking place when, cameras clicking, all the dear little mites wanted to have their photos taken.

'Now I know,' said Betsy in her ear when they arrived at the greenhouses—beautifully hot after the cold outside—where cucumbers were being grown.

'Know what?' Laurie asked.

'Well, you know how every Chinese we've seen wears only thin top clothing, yet they look like mini Incredible Hulks. Well, it's a question I've wanted to ask Mr Chan but haven't liked to—what do they wear underneath?' She pointed to an overhead rail. 'There you have it,' she said, drawing Laurie's attention to the thickest pair of long johns she had ever seen. 'The heat in here must have got too much for him.'

Laurie found the hospital they visited disappointing. She would like to have spoken with a doctor or a nurse, but there was no opportunity. They were hurried through corridor after corridor, all meaning very little except for her to be glad, however much it might be slated by the media, for her own country's health service. They were shown the pharmacy, which dealt with both Western and Chinese medicine, drawer upon drawer of herbs being on display.

They went to a restaurant for lunch, the meal was tasty, and Laurie was at last getting the hang of her chopsticks, eating her fair share from the many dishes brought to the table for them to help themselves. Fizzy orange and beer that Mr Dodd told her was very weak, were available to all.

'Where to this afternoon?' Laurie heard someone ask.

'Yet another temple,' she heard someone groan in reply, and had to smile. It was a bit like that.

'The Temple of Heaven,' Mr Chan informed them, when because of a few laggards they arrived late, 'was built by the Emperor Yong Le of the Ming Dynasty so that the Emperors could worship. We will go now to the Hall of Prayer.'

'Yet another Hall!' she heard that same voice groan, as they all trooped after Mr Chan to a round pagoda-like structure with triple deep blue tiled eaves, finished with a gold knob on top. It was surrounded by three circular white carved marble balustrades at three levels and reached by three flights of steps. The Hall was impressive in that it was built entirely without steel, cement or beams, and supported only on massive wooden pillars.

They were too late, apparently, to see the Echo Wall, and indeed the light was already begining to fade as Mr Chan took them to the Circular Mound Altar. And it was here that even the person who had groaned, 'Yet another

Hall!' took an interest, as Mr Chan explained how the three-tiered stone terrace was laid out in a geometrical design.

Maths not being her strong point, Laurie listened intently as their guide told them how in the old days the number nine was considered in China to be the most powerful number, so that the altar was constructed in multiples of nine.

His explanation began to make sense when they reached the top level, the third tier, open to the skies, and she saw that the stone slabs were laid so as to have nine at the centre, the next ring having eighteen and so on to the ninth and outer ring at the balustrade edge, which had eighty-one slabs in its construction, all single figures adding up to nine.

One or two of them laughed when it became obvious that she wasn't the only dud where maths were concerned, and elementary questions were put to Mr Chan, who was himself by this time growing confused. So they were all in good spirits by the time he told them that if one stood in the centre and said something in a whisper, the sound waves would reflect back from the balustrades so that not only would people around hear it clearly, but that it would bounce back more resonantly to the whisperer.

'Let me try!' Betsy was in there first. 'Mary had a little lamb,' she began without hesitation. 'Hey—it works!'

No sooner had she said it than everybody had to try it. But before it could come to Laurie's turn, Mr Chan was further instructing that if one person stood opposite another on the various slabs, they could whisper sounds to each other and both hear the reflected echo.

It was almost dusk by the time he was able to get them to leave the area, Shirley's cry of, 'I'm freezing!' having him saying that they must go to the bus now.

Finding she was last as the others began to troop down the steps, Laurie thought a couple of seconds more wouldn't matter if she nipped to the centre and tried the

'Mary had a little lamb' bit she had missed out on.

'Hesperus! the day is gone,' she began reciting, trying to be original. 'Soft falls the silent dew.'

'A tear is now on many a flower,' echoed back a voice—a voice that wasn't her own!—'And heaven lives with you.'

She spun round, that disturbed feeling Tyler aroused there as she recognised his voice even before in the failing light she recognised him. He was by himself, no sign of the rest of his group.

Though she knew she should go chasing after her own tour, surprise at seeing him had her rooted. Tyler didn't move either, but stood there, his expression unreadable in the dimness.

'Still mad at me, Lauretta Frost?' he asked softly, his voice reaching her clearly.

Was she still angry with him? She didn't know. She felt confused suddenly. 'How do you know my name?' she countered.

'You mean you don't know mine?' he mocked.

'I don't know your surname,' she replied. And when he didn't seem to see a need to supply it, she didn't want him thinking she had gone around making enquiries about him, 'Betsy said your name is Tyler.' He would know who Betsy was, everybody did.

'Good for Betsy,' he said—then startled her by saying, 'Are you anything at all like the young woman you're trying to make out you are?'

'What do you mean?' she asked, strangely not angry, but not knowing what he could mean.

'How much of you is the side of the female I've seen? The Lauretta whose only reason for letting me take her picture is because she thinks it will please her mother? The Lauretta who bothers to cart home a bottle of Moutai for her father because she thinks he might like to sample the Chinese brew?'

Dumbfounded that from what he had gleaned of her he

should think it out of keeping she should remember her parents while on holiday, Laurie could only stare through the gathering darkness at him. Then she was startled again when he said:

'Are you anything at all, Lauretta, like the young woman who's trying to give the impression that she's very careful about casual pick-ups—holiday romances?'

'Holiday romances!' she exclaimed, wondering what was happening to her that her temper was staying down.

Softly his voice reached her, and, her bewilderment growing, she saw he had moved until he was standing close up to her. 'We could have something going and you know it,' he said.

'I—I don't think I like you,' she stammered, when last night she had been sure she didn't.

'You don't have to like me,' came the silky reply. 'But you can't deny the attraction is there—for both of us.'

'I . . . .' She fought for words of denial, but they just wouldn't come. 'Wh-what did you mean just now—about me not being what I seem?' she asked instead.

His head was much too close to hers when he whispered, 'You don't know?' And before she could answer that mouth she had thought would be quite something was on hers, and he was kissing her for real this time.

There was that in her that wanted to resist, wanted to beat at his shoulders and tell him to stop, but that mobile mouth over hers was having the most disastrous effect on what she should be doing and what she wanted to do.

His mouth glided to her throat, felt warm as he brushed her polo collar away. Her hand bunched on his shoulder ready to push him away, but unfolded. It gripped, when his mouth returned to take hers, and before she knew it she was kissing him back, her arms around him. She was hot on a freezing cold night as his hands came round her, pressing her to him.

Again he kissed her, had her mindlessly responding,

kissing in return, moaning slightly that their clothes were a hindrance to a much closer contact—a wanton feeling attacking her of wanting to feel his body.

It was the sound of a voice calling her name, not Tyler's voice, but a female voice that had them breaking apart.

'Sounds as though you're being paged,' muttered Tyler in the darkness.

'Lauretta, is that you?' Betsy, peering at the two shapes standing close, had come to look for her.

'Just coming,' Laurie replied, her voice husky; where her brains were she didn't have any idea.

'Come on, then—the natives, hungry for their Peking duck supper, are getting restless!'

'G-goodbye,' Laurie managed, and left Tyler standing there as she hurried over to Betsy.

'Was that Tyler with you?' Betsy asked, before Laurie's brain could activate to think up excuses.

'Yes,' she replied quietly.

'You crafty thing,' said Betsy, the bus in sight, and her good humour restoring itself. 'There goes another one from my list!'

They had their Peking duck supper at a restaurant said to be famous for it. And even while Laurie was telling herself she would have felt hungry had the duck not been brought to the table complete with its head on, that to eat duck without recognising it as such would normally not bother her, but seeing it with its head on put her off the idea of eating it, she knew she was fooling herself.

That passionate encounter with Tyler had been more than instrumental in ruining her appetite, she had to face it. He had showed no aversion to a more intimate relationship—even while he was suspicious that she wasn't what she appeared to be, he still fancied her.

And what about her? The feelings he aroused in her from five or six kisses had shattered her. But it would be the utmost folly to give in to such feelings. He had said

she didn't have to like him—which meant of course that
he needn't necessarily like her either. What sort of basis
was that for any sort of relationship? Besides which, she
was returning to Hong Kong on Friday, the day after
tomorrow, and would never see him again after that.

It was still early when they returned to their hotel.
Laurie shut herself in her bedroom knowing that if Tyler
knocked on her door tonight, then she just didn't dare
trust herself to answer it.

Tyler did not knock on her door that night. And any
appetite that had wakened with her faded when she went
down to breakfast as she saw him seated with one or two
others from his party.

'Good morning,' she said in the general direction of his
table. She met his eyes briefly before she flicked her glance
away and wondered tetchily why, since she hadn't blushed
that she could remember since she was seventeen, hot
colour should choose that moment to crimson her face.

She was conscious that his tour were in front of hers
when they paid a visit to the Ming Tombs. It was a disappointing experience as far as she was concerned; the
mock-up of the burial coffins so much red-painted ply-
wood, the red paint carelessly smeared on to the beautiful
length of white marble on which they stood. This time,
though, whether she got separated from her group or not,
she contented herself with trailing behind rather than
come into contact with Tyler.

But having been careful to avoid contact with him,
Laurie found that evening, when her tour went with their
guide to a concert at the Workers' Stadium, that Tyler
had no intention of avoiding her.

The stadium was crowded as Mr Chan ushered them to
their places in the round auditorium that looked down into a
centre arena. Since she was first to go along their row, she was
at the end with only one vacant seat available.

That seat would have been occupied by Kay, she thought,

hoping her friend was now out of hospital and making a good recovery as her eyes scanned the rows in front where other Westerners sat, until she recognised someone from Tyler's group. So they were here! But where was he?

'Hello, Lauretta Frost,' said Tyler, coming from nowhere to calmly take the empty seat next to her.

Her insides started to act up, although she tried to keep her face expressionless. 'Your party are down there,' she said, half of her wanting him to go and find his right seat, the other half of her—wanting him to stay!

'The view's better up here,' he told her coolly, which had the desired effect of having her turn her head to look at him.

His eyes were on her, went to her mouth, a smile coming to his as though he was remembering some pleasurable experience. Laurie could no more stop her eyes from flicking to his mouth than fly, and her heart skipped a beat as that sensuous bottom lip curved.

'You arranged to sit here on purpose,' she accused, trying to get on top of the emotions he charged in her.

'Does that make you angry?'

It didn't. Useless to try and fool herself and say that it did, that she didn't like him, because that wasn't the way it was at all.

Mercifully she was saved a reply when the orchestra began to play. She turned to the front, trying to look as though she had forgotten he was sitting there, glued her eyes on the two male singers who were performing a duet.

Laurie did succeed in having her mind temporarily taken from him when, without regard to the entertainers giving their all down there on the floor, spectators came in and out the whole time, not unlike a rugger crowd at a match she had once gone to with her brother Jamie. No one was hushing anyone else, she saw, when anyone felt the need for conversation, the Chinese eating their way through fruit, sweets and chocolate and anything else they had thought to bring with them the whole of the time.

Mr Chan sat in the middle of their group translating when a pair of comedians took the floor, but Laurie was not close enough to pick up what he was saying.

The lights in the auditorium were full on, and had not dimmed at all as the various performers went through their routines. But they did go down when a male ballet dancer came on to perform, a green spotlight picking out his grace and movement.

And that was the moment that she became more conscious than ever of Tyler sitting next to her. Not that he moved, but she felt an intimacy with him; his topcoat like hers was on his lap, touching her legs. She felt stifled, wanting to brush his coat away, wanting those lights on again.

Eventually the dancer finished his routine and the lights came on. With relief Laurie began to feel somewhere near normal again. But she couldn't any longer forget the man sitting next to her.

A male singer was next to perform, Mr Chan translating the song for those who could hear him.

'He's singing of a girl he has seen and wants to get to know,' said Tyler, seeing, she thought, that Mr Chan's voice wasn't reaching her. 'He's telling the story of a girl who pretends she doesn't want to know him, but who he thinks does.'

Tyler had a nice voice, Laurie thought, glad his smattering of Mandarin extended this far so that she could enjoy the song.

'Her beautiful skin delights his eyes,' he went on. 'Her figure puts Venus to shame. The daintiness of her nose delights him, the charm and allure of her lips invite him.'

Laurie was on the way to forgetting the singer as the music of Tyler's voice filled her ears. That was until he said:

'Never has he seen such wonderful green eyes, hair that shines red, making him want to bury his face in its glory . . . .'

Swiftly she turned, turned and saw his eyes were on her. 'Are you flirting with me?' she asked, unable to believe the Chinese singer could be singing of a green-eyed, redheaded Chinese girl.

'The girl has brains as well as beauty,' Tyler drawled, and Laurie turned away.

She guessed the concert was about to end when regardless of the performance still going on, hordes of Chinese on the opposite side of the auditorium got up and started to exit. And when the act finished and all the entertainers came out to bow, Mr Chan stood up and so did the rest of her party.

Struggling to get into her coat, knowing it was going to be bitter outside, Laurie felt Tyler's hands come to assist her with it. She half turned to thank him, then felt him turning her to face him.

'Mustn't let you catch a chill,' he said, and had started to button up her coat for her before she could turn away.

Her coat was new, the buttonholes stiff still, but he forced a button through easily enough, his fingers brushing her breast as he did up the one below her neck button. Her insides quivered, although she knew his touch was unintentional.

'I'll do the rest,' shot from her in a nerve-full moment.

It brought his eyes to stare down into hers, his expression slightly mocking. 'Don't be impatient, I'm going as fast as I can,' he told her coolly. And in view of that, aware she had been short with him in the past, Laurie let her hands fall.

'Thank you,' she muttered when he had finished. Then she turned, alarm spearing that she couldn't see any of her group around and that she didn't have any idea where her bus was. 'They've gone!' she exclaimed, her anxiety showing.

'There's no need to panic.'

His voice was soothing. But he didn't understand. 'I get lost in strange places,' she said quickly. 'I always have done.'

She was already speeding along the row ready to chase in the direction she thought they had gone, but a hand on her shoulder stayed her.

'No need to break into a trot. They'll wait for you.'

'But I don't know where they are!' she said, seeing he still didn't understand.

'I'll help you look,' he said, talking calmly to her as out of the row he walked by her side. 'If the worst comes to the worst you can always have a lift back with my lot.' And, trying to get her to smile, 'I'll even let you sit on my lap, since there aren't any spare seats.'

But Laurie couldn't see anything to smile at. 'What if your bus has gone too?'

'Then we'll take a taxi.'

But she didn't want that either. Already Tyler had got to her. She wanted to be back with the others where she would feel safe. Even while she admitted she no longer disliked him, there was still that something about him that had her feeling threatened. She didn't want it to be just him and her in a taxi and that long drive back.

'I want to go by bus,' she said mulishly.

But she discovered as he took her from the stadium, past throngs of milling people, that the person who must have been born with her share of sense of direction must be him, for in a very few minutes after that he was escorting her to the door of her bus.

She turned to give him her heartfelt thanks, her breathing easier now she had reached sanctuary. 'Thank you so much, Tyler,' she began.

'Any time,' he replied, and strode away.

'I'm definitely going to cross someone off my list,' Betsy remarked across the aisle with a grin as they set off. Then promptly forgetting everything as her head swivelled round, she said loud enough for everyone to hear, 'Hey, I've just noticed, with all these thousands of cyclists dodging the bus, none of the bikes have lights!'

'I noticed that before,' said Burt. 'Mr Chan says there are three million bicycles in Peking.'

'I wonder what the accident rate is,' said Mrs Dodd, and straightaway called on their guide to tell them.

What his answer was Laurie never knew. Away from Tyler she was at last coming to terms with the truth that had to be faced. The truth of why she had been overwhelmingly aware of him from the very beginning. The truth of why she had tried to dislike him from the start. That something in her that had her feeling threatened, that something that had known there would be pain for her from knowing him. Quite simply—she was in love with him.

They were all up early the next morning to fly to Canton. A brief stop there, then a twenty-five-minute flight to Hong Kong. With some of the group still half asleep it was a quiet bus load of people who travelled to the airport in Peking.

Laurie too should have been still tired, for she had slept very little last night. But the hope of seeing Tyler, the man she loved without so much as knowing his last name, kept her awake and alert-eyed as she sought to find him in the waiting area.

She saw one of his group and hope rose. Saw him, and looked the other way her heart pounding. She moaned inwardly at the times she had fired up at him, moaning at the missed chances she'd had to get to know him better.

Oh, what was the use of moaning? she thought, wanting desperately to take another look at him but afraid her face would give her away. Tyler had been ready for a holiday romance, he had as good as told her so, but it wasn't just a holiday romance she wanted. She wanted it to go on long past her holiday, wanted it to be for ever.

Either he didn't see her or he had decided that since his holiday was over there was no point in trying to further their relationship. That meant, of course, she thought, hurt, that all that had been in his mind was a physical relationship with her.

Disappointment in him hit her as she saw then that

with all chance of getting her into bed with him gone, Tyler must think it a waste of time to bother with her any more.

Betsy had a seat by her on the Ilyushin 62 plane, leaving her sister to sit with Mervyn. 'Thought you'd be sitting with Tyler,' she chirruped in her cheerful way.

'He's not on our tour,' was the best Laurie could do.

'That wouldn't have bothered me,' said Betsy, giving her a serious look. 'Had a fight?'

'No, nothing like that.'

'Do you want me to go and tell him there's a vacant seat here?' she offered. 'I don't mind moving.'

'No!' shot from Laurie as she cringed from the very idea.

'All right, all right, don't get knotted up,' the Australian girl laughed goodhumouredly. 'I was only trying to help. Though how you can bear not to have another crack at snaffling the best-looking bachelor I've seen in all my nineteen years, I don't know. You seemed to be doing fine too from what I could see . . . .'

'Bachelor?' Laurie picked up, the ghastly thought coming to her that Tyler could have been married for all she knew.

'He hasn't been kidding you he's got a wife, has he?' And when Laurie shook her head, Betsy went on to say, 'Good. I should hate to think he lied when I asked him why he hadn't brought his wife along.'

'What did he say?' She couldn't hold the question in, much as she wanted Betsy to think she wasn't interested in him.

'He gave me one of those smiles that make your bones melt,' Laurie knew what she meant, 'and told me he wasn't married, but that as charming as he found me would I keep out of his hair because he had other things on his mind.'

'He said that?' Laurie could see him saying it, and thought he must have delivered it with some charm that the younger girl's feelings obviously weren't wounded, because she appeared quite happy about it.

'Hmm,' Betsy agreed. 'You were the other 'thing' he had on his mind, of course. But I didn't see that until I saw you and him together at the echo place. I thought then that he must be keen, because the rest of his tour went somewhere else, so he must have made a special trip to come after you.'

'I don't think so,' Laurie began, thinking it could have been in his mind to go anywhere, it was coincidental he had ended up at the Circular Mound Altar. But Betsy had spotted something from the window where Burt was sitting and was out of her seat before she could say more.

Pride demanded she didn't 'see' Tyler when they disembarked at Canton. Her interest in what their guide had to tell them about the visit, not on their itinerary, to a Memorial Park dedicated to the heroes of the 1927 uprising had never been more avid.

But her heart was heavy as she boarded the bus that was to take them to fill in a few hours before their flight to Hong Kong took off. She would never see Tyler again, went her thoughts as, unable to become enchanted with Canton, she stared pensively out of the window. There was a possibility his group would visit the Memorial Park too, might even be on the same flight to Hong Kong. But in her heart she had said goodbye to him.

Promises to write and keep in touch had already been made within her group. From what she could make out all of them were spending only one night in Hong Kong before they took their flights home. She didn't even know where Tyler lived, what work he did. In fact, her thoughts went on, she barely knew him at all, and yet—as much as she didn't want it to be—she had fallen in love with him. Sense disappeared when the heart became involved, she thought, unable to see any sense in what had happened to her.

It was a relief to her when they arrived at the park,

and their guide advised them that the bus would be driven round to the exit the other side, and that they had a whole half an hour to wander in the park as they pleased.

'Free at last!' Betsy whooped when the guide was out of earshot, for it was seldom they had gone anywhere without a guide in tow. 'See you later,' she called, and was off.

As was everybody else, Laurie saw. Mr and Mrs Dodd went in the direction of some buildings, Shirley with Mervyn's arm about her making for some steps. Laurie wanted to be on her own too, but mindful of her erring feet, she headed in the direction the guide had said the other exit would be.

It was peaceful in the park after the blare of car horns outside. Someone had said there was no private transport in China, only taxis and official cars, but if that were true then they certainly made their presence known.

Music interspersed with something being said in Chinese from time to time came over a loudspeaker. But as she wandered through trees and shrubs, and went over to see a lake that drew her attention, as it was not frozen like those in Peking, Laurie fell in with the peace of the scene.

Several times something attracted her away from the walkways, but each time after going to see a particular shrub or, a display of chrysanthemums set out in pots in a paved area, she would return back to the path.

That was until she spotted a type of shrub she had never seen before, near to a concrete flight of steps. Fascinated, she looked, and looked again, spending minutes turning the leaves this way and that. Never before had she seen a leaf that shone healthily bright green on the top and bright red on the underside.

It was too much for her trigger finger to resist. She undid her camera case, snapped off shots from every angle, then neared the shrub to touch once more that splendid leaf.

Quite when she became conscious that someone was watching her she didn't know, but suddenly her head jerked up—and there on the steps stood Tyler! He was looking at her, but did not make any move to come forward. And in that instant she knew he had said goodbye to her too.

She was walking away from him, hurrying in amongst the trees, not pausing until it came to her some minutes later that with Tyler having written 'the end' to the attraction he had said they both felt for each other, she had no need to worry that he would come chasing after her.

She realised too then, as she clenched her teeth against tears her saddened thoughts would have her shedding, that the walkway she had so far kept in sight was now nowhere to be seen.

She tried not to panic; the bus wouldn't go without her, as Tyler had remarked last night. Forget Tyler—she brought her mind back. Concentrate. She walked on for another five minutes heading, she was sure, in the direction opposite from where the entrance was.

And then, relief surging, she saw the exit. Not a wide entrance like the one she had come in by, still it was the exit she was looking for. It was an iron-railed meshed gate, she saw when she neared it, and there was a cluster of khaki-clad men standing by it, the red star in the middle of their caps denoting that they were soldiers.

'Excuse me. Thank you,' she said, and smiled, as they moved out of the way to let her through. She knew they didn't understand a word, but didn't see why she shouldn't do her best to further East–West relations the same as Tyler h . . . Oh, damn Tyler!

Outside the gate she found herself in a wide street. Looking up the road, she spotted the bus in the distance and checked her watch. Half an hour exactly. Given there were a few laggards in her group with any luck she might be first back, she thought. Then she grew concerned as she neared the stationary bus that it didn't look quite like the bus that had brought them to the park.

It wasn't the same bus, she saw when she neared it. She was beside it when, still hopeful that it might be, she peered in to search the seat that should have held her coat, dispensed with since Canton's climate was more similar to the sixteen degrees centigrade of Hong Kong than the freezing temperature of Peking.

Her coat was not there, confirming that it was not her bus. Looking further up the road, she saw a bend in the road. Having come this far she decided it would be silly not to carry on, to reach that bend and look to see if the bus holding her coat was tucked away around the corner.

Laurie grew hot and sticky as she hurried on. As she had a tee-shirt on beneath the thick sweater she had needed to don that morning, her sweater was soon off and over her arm. But she was still hot as she came to the corner, going a little way down the new street, but hope died when she saw there wasn't a bus in sight.

There was a stitch in her side and it seemed to her that she had hurried a couple of miles, but there was nothing for it, she would have to hurry back the way she had come, go past the gate she had come out from and investigate that way.

She checked her watch again as she passed the gate. Already she was half an hour adrift, she saw, getting more and more worried. Memory of their guide saying they would have lunch before returning to the airport picked at her as she rounded another corner, and still no bus in sight. The thought of a bus load of people having to go without their lunch because of her nagged at her when, admitting defeat, she knew there was no way she was going to find them, that they would have to come looking for her.

Memory stirred of her father saying to her, 'When you get lost'—not, '*If* you get lost,' they knew her of old— 'always try to get back to the place you started from, we'll start looking there.'

She had better get back inside the park, she thought, and started back again, making for the gate she had exited from. She saw an opening that might have taken her into the park, but it looked small and she didn't dare risk it.

At last she reached the iron-railed gate. But when she tried to open it she found it locked, and realised only then that she shouldn't be where she was anyway. She had never been meant to come out of that exit, she saw. It had just been her ghastly luck that she had reached that gate just as the soldiers had unlocked it to come through. They had let her go through presumably because they hadn't seen any reason why she shouldn't, but had then seen to it that the gate was properly locked afterwards.

Laurie remembered the small opening she had passed, and knew she would have to risk it. She had to get back inside that park somehow.

It did lead into the park, she discovered some five minutes later, and a small feeling of relief entered her fretting soul that at least she had got this far.

Very carefully she went through the tall trees, anxiety her companion. She heard the Chinese music she had heard before and kept her eyes about her as she went steadily on. The music stopped, but she was hardly aware of it.

Then she too stopped—stopped and stood rooted. For the message following the music wasn't being broadcast in Chinese—it was being broadcast in English. And given that the equipment being used distorted the voice slightly, Laurie knew she would know that voice anywhere. It was Tyler's voice.

CHAPTER FIVE

UNABLE to move at first, so great was the shock of hearing not only an English voice when she had been expecting to hear a Chinese one, and that after all those worrying miles she must have walked that voice was Tyler's, she listened intently to what he was saying.

'Take it easy, Laurie,' his voice was even, washing away her panic. 'The bus won't go without you.'

It was so good to hear him she nearly burst into tears there and then. But she couldn't give way, for he was going on to instruct her:

'There are probably few places you'll remember if you're as upset as I think you are. But make for the big flight of steps where I last saw you.' He broke off, giving her time in case she didn't recall instantly. 'You know the steps I mean—the steps by the red and green-leafed shrub.' A pause again, then so comfortingly. 'Don't worry if you can't find them. Just stay in the park—I'll find you.'

Laurie went perhaps five steps forward, then stopped. She turned slowly about, her eyes searching, knowing that even while thinking she was going the right way, she could well be wrong. And then there to the right of her she saw what had been hidden a few yards back. It looked like concrete. She moved hurriedly in that direction, her heart lifting as more concrete in the shape of a step appeared, two steps, three. And there was her red and green-leafed shrub.

Though she had thought she was too exhausted to run, her feet picked up speed, only to slow again as the trees thinned. For there—and her tears wanted to spurt once more—was Tyler advancing from the opposite direction.

'Tyler!' she tried to call his name. But her throat was dry, a whisper leaving her that no one would have heard, certainly not the man she loved who hadn't yet seen her.

Her legs felt weak as she came out of the trees and stood on concrete, Tyler with his back to her as he turned to scan the way he had come.

'Tyler,' she said again, and this time he heard.

He turned, saw her weary face that anxiety had paled, her breasts rising and falling, the sweater over her arm. And then in a few strides he was up close to her.

'Poor little love,' he said, oh, so gently that the tears sprang to her eyes. 'Has it been a rotten time for you?'

'Oh, Tyler!' she cried, and felt this was the nearest to heaven she had ever been, when without another word he gathered her safely in his arms.

How many minutes they stayed like that, her head against his chest as she fought with all she had not to cry all over him, his strong arms holding her close to his heart, she couldn't have said. But at last he was putting her away from him. 'Feel better now?' he asked, still in that same gentle voice.

She nodded, afraid to speak in case the feeling of tears inside had her voice carrying a sob in it. Whether Tyler saw the battle against tears she was having she didn't know, but his voice was teasing when next he spoke.

'We'll have to get you fitted with some electronic homing device,' he told her, that bone-melting smile on his face.

'Th-thank you for finding me,' she tried, her voice fairly steady although there was a husky note to it. Then, as memory returned, 'You called me Laurie!' she exclaimed, liking that in her moment of crisis his voice had added a friendliness to it with him dropping the formal-sounding Lauretta.

'Did I?' he said, his eyes hooded for a moment so she

wished she knew what he was thinking. 'Do you mind?'

She smiled. 'I like it,' she said, 'Everybody at home calls me Laurie.'

He looked away from her, and her smiled faded. The terrible thought occurred—did he think she was presuming from the fact that he had bothered to come looking for her that he might want to see her when they were both back in England?

'We'd better get you back to your bus,' he said, the gentleness gone. But for all he was still sounding friendly, Laurie's pride was dying a thousand deaths that he might think she was chasing him.

'Ready when you are,' she said, keeping her voice carefully even, but not daring to lead the way since she still didn't know where the bus was.

'Good girl,' he said. And if that was supposed to be a compliment that he had seen how she had mastered her tears, as she fell into step with him Laurie was feeling too chilled to appreciate it.

At the airport she felt too upset to be anything but quiet. Her apology for keeping them waiting had been met with smiles and comments of, 'Don't worry about it.' But she still felt the burden of guilt for the way they had rushed their lunch.

'Cheer up.' Betsy came over to where they were all standing about as though waiting for something to happen. 'If you're still feeling down because you were late, don't be. Half a dozen of us got lost—I only made it back to the bus thirty minutes before you did myself.'

'Did you?' Laurie felt some of the weight of guilt lift. Then she remembered the galloping feast lunch had been.

'And we needn't have bolted our meal anyway, 'Betsy went on. 'We've been kicking about here for twenty minutes now with nothing happening.' She broke off. 'Hello, there's something going on over there!' She was off, to come back again, her eyes searching for her sister as she told Laurie, 'We can go and change our money,' and as an afterthought, 'You know we're not allowed to take Chinese currency out of the country?'

Laurie did know, but before she could say so, Betsy was off again, having spotted Shirley.

Thinking some activity wouldn't come amiss, Laurie decided to change her remaining yuan into Hong Kong dollars. Her Hong Kong wallet was in her case, but she had sufficient Chinese currency to exchange for her taxi fare to Mei Lai's without her bothering to go scrabbling in her case to change another travellers cheque before she took her case through Customs. She had meant to take the wallet out of her case this morning, but thoughts of the unwanted love that had grown in her for Tyler had made her forget it.

She stood up abruptly, and tried to escape from thoughts of him by concentrating her thoughts on Mei Lai and how she would see her when she finished work. She hoped she would like the silk scarf she had bought her.

Laurie reached the desk; an elderly man in front of her was being attended to, and she was just delving into her bag for her purse when she thought she was hearing things.

'I trust you're fully recovered from getting lost, Lauretta.'

'You're going to Hong Kong on the same plane!' came from her as she turned and saw Tyler. Since he had shot off in a taxi after seeing her to her bus she had for no reason thought he was staying on.

'I have business there.'

'Oh,' she said, dearly wanting to know what his business was. Wanting to know anything about him that would give her an insight into the man who held her heart. 'This has been a working holiday for you, then?'

'A bit of both,' he replied, which told her nothing.

It was her turn to be served. She handed over the yuan, fen, and the light silvery-coloured coins, and was satisfied with the hundred-dollar bill she received in change. She would still have fifty or sixty dollars left after she had paid her taxi, she calculated. For Mei Lai lived in the Western District of Hong Kong, and there was the toll fare to pay for crossing under the tunnel from Kowloon to Hong Kong.

She came away from the desk, too much aware of Tyler being near as she mentally converted the fifty or sixty dollars into four or five pounds sterling. She went and stood near her case, expecting any moment now to be going through Customs. Then she noticed things were buzzing at another desk, and was grateful it had given her something to say, for though she was usually at ease in male company, the most tonguetied feeling of shyness came over her when Tyler, pushing notes inside his wallet, came and stood by her.

'What's going on over there?' she asked in a rush.

He turned to see where she was indicating. 'Paying over airport tax, by the look of it.'

She had forgotten all about airport tax—if she ever knew. 'Does it have to be paid in Chinese money?' she asked him, thinking he would think her an utter fool if she had to go back to the currency desk and change her money back again.

'You've cashed in all your Chinese money?' he guessed, a suggestion of a smile lighting his face.

'I can easily change it back again,' she said, wondering why when she was efficient at most things she did, Tyler only ever seemed to see the side of her that made her look stupid.

'No need, I've enough yuan for the two of us.'

She liked that, the way he said 'the two of us', but she was used to paying her own way. 'Can you change a hundred-dollar note?' She hoped the airport tax wasn't going to consume all of that. 'I haven't got anything smaller on me.'

'I'll treat you,' he said, and smiled. 'It's only five yuan, after all.'

To press the point would have made her look less sophisticated than she wanted him to think she was. 'Thank you,' she said, and left it at that as she went with him to settle the airport tax, a feeling of happiness in her that she was having these few bonus minutes with him.

As soon as the airport tax was paid a general movement was made towards Customs. Laurie picked up her coat from off her case, then reached to pick up her case. Her fingers tingled as they connected with Tyler's. 'I'll carry it for you,' he said obligingly, unaware that just the touch of his skin on hers did crazy things to her insides.

He wasn't averse to conversation as they stood waiting their turn, asking her if she was staying in Hong Kong just the one night as almost everyone else was doing, or would she be staying longer.

Hope she couldn't still was in her that since he had mentioned that he had business in Hong Kong he might be staying on too. Hope that perhaps he had it in mind to ask her out.

'I shall be there until next Thursday,' she told him, her heart racing excitedly.

'You're staying in a hotel in Hong Kong or Kowloon?' he queried.

Was he asking so she could tell him the name of her hotel? Her heartbeats went into overdrive. 'I'm not staying at a hotel. I'm staying with a friend—in Hong Kong itself,' she tacked on.

How did she give him Mei Lai's address without him asking for it? A dreadful thought occurred to her when he didn't follow it up.

'A girl friend,' she said quickly, in case he had gleaned

other ideas about the sex of the 'friend' she was to stay with.

'You have many friends in Hong Kong?' he asked. 'People you've arranged to see during your visit?'

Wanting badly to tell him that all her days were free from now until next Thursday, she realised he would soon see how eager she was to see him again if she did that. Besides which, she had no idea if Mei Lai had arranged anything for this weekend.

'I've got nothing arranged at the moment,' she said, going as far as she could. 'My friend might have something planned for us this weekend,' and in a rush suddenly, 'But since Mei Lai is a working girl, my days will be fairly free, I imagine.'

Knowing what she had said had still come out as giving him an open invitation to contact her, Laurie couldn't be sorry. And then it was her turn with the Customs officer. Her mind more on Tyler than anything, she hadn't any idea what the Customs man was asking, until Tyler, his mind more on the Chinese than her, apparently, told her the man was asking for the declaration of jewellery they had all had to complete before entering the country.

'Oh yes,' she said, managing to feel inadequate again, sure she would not have felt so had Tyler not been standing right by her shoulder.

She delved in her bag and found the carbon copy declaration they had allowed her to keep and handed it to the official, keeping her mind concentrated on him as he made signs that he wanted to see her jewellery.

She smiled at him as she showed him the gold chain that encircled her throat. The smile was still on her face when with a further dip into her bag she extracted the ring box Maurice had given her and opened it to show the man she hadn't parted with any jewellery while she had been in his country.

Then abruptly her smile disappeared, and shock hit

her at the pure aggression she heard spilling from Tyler as he too saw the ring with its unusual setting.

'Where the *hell* did you get that?' he barked.

'Where . . .!'

For a moment she was so shaken by the change from his smiling attitude to this snarling man that her own anger didn't surface. But as his voice sorted itself out in her brain as being accusing, just as though he thought she had stolen it, her ire stirred itself.

'I didn't steal it,' she flashed back.

'Nor did you get it for *good behaviour*,' he bit rudely.

'Why, you . . . .' she started to fire. Then through the heat of her temper came a thought that had her checking. 'I—I'm not engaged,' she said, more quietly, pure wonder starting in her that he might think she was, and was angry because. . . .

'Nor likely to be, to . . . .'

'Thank you very much,' she cut off his 'my way of thinking' she was certain he was about to add, glad of anger again to hide her hurt.

She turned from him, choking back tears. Oh, what foolish dreams! There she was, all starry-eyed about him, and he, the bad-tempered brute, had just as good as told her that their acquaintanceship was going nowhere—certainly that he for one would never consider the idea of being engaged to her.

She smiled at the official, hoping he hadn't been left with any lasting impression that the English were a race who could change at the drop of a coolie hat from smiling to looking ready to cut each other's throats, and went to stand in line at the passport check.

She knew Tyler had come to stand behind her, but wouldn't look at him as she went to the farthest emigration officer, who took her passport from her and enquired, 'Stamp?'

'Yes, please,' she answered, having heard that some

people preferred not to have the stamp of some countries endorsed in their passports because it presented difficulties when going into other countries who weren't on friendly terms with that particular nation.

She tried to pretend Tyler wasn't there as she waited for her document to be checked, then smiled again as the Chinese, practising his English, handed back her passport and charmingly smiled as he said, 'Thank you, Miss Flost.'

She was about to turn away when she heard Tyler getting the same treatment. 'Thank you, Mr Glay,' she heard, and went to the departure lounge having learned that if the R in Tyler's name had been mispronounced as hers had been, then his name was Gray.

Tyler Gray, she thought, still sore from his last remarks to her as she sat in the Trident on the short flight to Hong Kong. Well, there wasn't any doubt about it now, that once the plane had landed, she had seen the last of him.

With or without her address, it was over. Over before it had begun. 'Nor likely to be,' he had snarled when she had told him she wasn't engaged, and that hurt. How could she have fallen in love with such an ungracious swine? Even if he didn't fancy her enough to make it permanent, there had been no need to yell it at her so that anybody could have heard it.

A line of a poem she had read somewhere, 'And love me still but know not why,' came to her, and she couldn't help but agree. For even having seen that nasty side to him, she still loved him, and she had no idea why either.

Oh, to hell with him, she thought, as the need to explain all about that ring to him crept in. Why should she? Who was he to stand in moral judgement on how she had got the ring? It could have been given to her by a wealthy relative for all he knew—and that hurt her pride too, that to him she must look as though she didn't have a wealthy relative to her name. She didn't—but he wasn't to know that. It was beneath her now to so much as bring up the subject of the ring after what he had said. And anyway, why was she wasting her time with such thoughts? She wasn't going to see him again, was she—that was a fact.

Because everyone was saying goodbye to everyone else when they collected their luggage, her brief glance at Tyler as he hefted up his case from the conveyor belt was the last Laurie saw of him. For her second glance at where he had been showed he had disappeared. Desperate for another look at him, she craned to see him, but he was nowhere in sight.

'You've got my address,' said Betsy, suitcase in hand as she walked with her to where some of the party were going to catch a taxi. 'Though since I'll be home before you I'll most likely write first. But we must keep in touch. Perhaps you'll be able to come over and stay with us some time?'

'I'd like that,' Laurie told her, glad to have other food for her thoughts. 'Though since it's going to take me ages to save up you'll probably make it to England before I make it to Australia.'

'And you can introduce me to your brother James,' said the incorrigble Betsy, having shared details of her family and heard something of Laurie's over the last six days.

'You'll like each other, I feel sure,' Laurie said with a smile. James was a chatterbox too.

'I didn't see Tyler go, did you?' Betsy asked, as they passed through a crowd of people waiting to greet friends and relatives.

'He just took his case and disappeared,' said Laurie, trying to speak conversationally, as though his abrupt departure meant nothing to her.

'He'd got the hump on the plane,' Betsy offered. 'I went to have a chat to him, but I could tell from the disgruntled look on his face that he wasn't up to being sociable. Have you two had a row?'

'I shouldn't think anything I could say to him would upset him,' Laurie replied offhandedly.

'He's pretty self-sufficient, isn't he?' Betsy agreed.

The others doubled up in taxis to get to their hotels. And it was as Laurie got into the taxi that would take her through the cross-harbour tunnel and to Mei Lai's home that, with her skin prickling, she felt sure she saw the man she had thought was following her that day she had visited the Hong Kong Museum. She twisted round in her seat as her taxi pulled away, but the bald-headed man wasn't anywhere to be seen.

Don't start imagining you're being followed again, she thought, having forgotten about that wretched ring for the last few days—had so forgotten her fears about it, she had been quite unthinking of its value when she had pulled it out to show that official in Canton.

Bother the ring! Bother Tyler Gray, she thought unhappily. It was for sure he wasn't fretting about her— why should she fret about him? If he had such a low opinion of her that he could say what he had about her marriage prospects, then he could go to the devil! And anyway, no man was going to have her sitting in the back of a taxi crying.

She wiped a stray tear from her eye as the taxi came out of the tunnel, telling herself if she did happen to bump into Tyler Gray during her stay, then without doubt she was going to look straight through him.

Hong Kong was as noisy and bustling as it had been before. But that sense of inner happiness she had felt just by being there was sadly absent, as the nightmare traffic hit her anew, a reminder that she would have to get used to crossing its teeming roads again.

The streets were still so much a jumble to her. But when the taxi turned off and headed for the dockland area, Laurie at last began to recognise sights that were familiar to her.

She paid the driver, saw her hundred-dollar bill had dwindled and thought as she waited for him to get her case from the trunk that since she didn't know what plans Mei Lai had made for the evening, she would pause only to drop her case in, extract her wallet with her traveller's cheques, and nip along to the bank so she could pay her share of the expenses should they be going out that night.

Laurie smiled at the concierge as she went in, having no need this time to ask him for the keys—he having been previously authorised by Mei Lai to hand them over—because she still had the keys with her.

She took the lift to Mei Lai's floor, inserted one key in the gate that each flat had just in front of the door which enabled tenants to keep their apartments secure when in the heat of summer they needed to have the main door open to allow the air to circulate.

She slid the gate back, inserting the other key in the main door, then pushed it inward as she turned to pick up her case. Setting her case inside as she concentrated on getting the iron gate shut, Laurie had no need to look into the room.

The gate closed and the wooden door secured, she went to bend to pick up her case. Then her world went crazy.

She blinked, not believing what her eyes were telling her, and felt the colour leave her that her eyes were still sending back that same picture.

'*You*!' she gasped, and still couldn't believe it.

For the tall man standing there, dressed in sports shirt and slacks, was a man she had last seen at Kai Tak airport. The man she had thought never to see again—none other than Tyler Gray!

CHAPTER SIX

'You!' Laurie exclaimed again, her head spinning. So stunned was she to see him there, she had checked the keys in her hand to see she hadn't come to the wrong flat, before she realised she wouldn't have been able to get in if those keys did not fit. 'What are you doing here?' She stared at him, her shock written plainly across her face.

The expression on Tyler's face must have been the same disgruntled one Betsy had witnessed on the plane, she thought, as he retaliated with:

'I might well ask you the same question.'

All Laurie's pride rose to the surface at what she saw as a suggestion that he thought she was following him.

'This happens to be my friend's flat,' she flared. 'This is where I'm staying.'

'Now isn't that just great,' he drawled sarcastically, and further stunned her by adding, 'So am I.'

'You can't be . . .!' she started to exclaim, still in shock at finding him there. Her brain wasn't yet up to sorting out how, in all of Hong Kong, Tyler Gray came to think he would be staying in the very same private residence as she herself.

Then the sarcasm of his words hit her, to blot out all thought save that clearly he had gone off all idea of any relationship with her. That hurt, stiffened her, that from at one time definitely not being averse, he now considered her a cross he had to bear until such time as one or the other of them left.

'There's no room here for you,' she said sharply, looking away so he shouldn't see her hurt. She stared round the tiny flat, wondering where he thought he was going to

sleep since the bedroom was about the size of her parents'
coalhouse back home and had little space in it for more
than the double bunk in there. And she and Mei Lai
were going to have those bunk beds, she thought, aggression rising.

Her eyes went to the small two-seater settee and
registered that he would never get his length in there.
She turned her face back to him, saw his eyes had
followed her glance to the settee, and saw him shake his
head.

'No way,' he told her bluntly.

'But there's only one bedroom,' she protested, 'and Mei
Lai and I are having that.' Then, the shock of everything
that was happening clearing, 'You never said you knew
Mei Lai when I mentioned her name in Canton.'

'I should imagine there's more than one Chinese girl
with that name,' he told her sardonically, adding, 'although none of them are known to me.'

'You don't know Mei Lai?' Her usually quick-thinking
brain, that had been shocked, was now making up for its
temporary dormant state. 'Then why are you here? If
Mei Lai hasn't given you permission. . . .' She stopped,
fears about the safety of Anona's ring back with her. Oh
God, she didn't want to believe Tyler was a crook, but he
had seen that ring at the airport, and by his harsh exclamation had obviously guessed its worth straight
away. . . .

'I have every right to be here,' he butted into her
thoughts. Then, looking fed up that he should have to
bother to explain anything to her, but that seeming to be
the only way this argument was going to be got quickly
out of the way, 'There's obviously been some foul-up. I'm
in Hong Kong partly on business. . . .'

'You told me that,' she interrupted, her suspicions not
yet ready to be allayed.

'I'm a buyer,' he went on, ignoring her as if she hadn't

spoken, 'here to see some people who are anxious to do business with the firm I represent. So anxious are they to sell to us that when word filtered through how intensely I dislike living in hotels, the head of the firm arranged this flat for me.'

'But this is Mei Lai's flat!'

'So you said,' he rapped shortly. 'Which leads me to ask—what firm does she work for?'

'The Ting Yat Electronic Company,' Laurie said promptly.

'The same firm I'm here to see,' Tyler told her.

It was starting to make sense—or was it? What he had said so far sounded convincing, but surely Mei Lai, even for the sake of her firm securing a large order, wouldn't have agreed to share her flat with some unknown man! Though—doubt began to trickle in—Mei Lai must be used to overcrowding as most Hong Kong people were, so perhaps she had thought one more wouldn't make any difference? But surely, Laurie thought, sending doubt on its way, surely she would have seen her firm weren't likely to get an order if the man they were hoping to impress had to spend his nights cramped up on that settee?

That settled it for her. 'I'm sure Mei Lai wouldn't have agreed to such a thing,' she told him tartly.

'There's only one way to find out,' he said confidently. 'Give her a ring.'

'I don't know her number,' she said, feeling stupid again.

Then she discovered that to Tyler's smattering of Mandarin she could add Cantonese, as giving her a look that said he agreed she was stupid and that he was fed up to the back teeth with her, he picked up the phone and rang directory enquiries.

'Perhaps you can make yourself useful and jot the number down,' he suggested disagreeably while he waited.

Fuming suddenly, Laurie searched in her bag, and was ready, pencil poised, when he relayed the number before putting down the phone.

'Your turn,' he told her, pointing to the instrument.

Wanting to hit him over the head with it, Laurie picked up the phone and dialled the number he had given her. Then she was made madder that the telephonist didn't seem to understand her when she asked to speak to Mei Lai, and offered her a flood of Cantonese in return, that told Laurie she was going to have to enlist Tyler's help.

She held out the phone, refusing to feel a fool that she didn't speak Cantonese. 'Will you tell them I want to speak to Mei Lai Wong, please,' she said, wishing her Chinese friend was here and not at work so she could sort the whole muddle out.

Listening to Tyler speaking, Laurie saw he was probably skilled in several languages, since from what he had said, he must be an international buyer. But the longer he spoke, making no move to hand the phone back to her so she could talk personally to Mei Lai, the more concerned Laurie became.

She was right to be concerned, she discovered some minutes later. For instead of handing the phone back to her as she was expecting, she heard him say, '*Joy geen*.' which she knew from her guide book meant goodbye, and saw him put the phone back on its rest.

'Apparently,' he said, thrusting his hands in his pockets, and managing to look casual although his face was stern, 'Mei Lai Wong is still in China.'

'China? She can't be!' Stupefied, Laurie stared at him. 'She had only one week due to her, and she had that my first week here.' Her mind boggling, Laurie wondered if between them she and the Chinese girl had got the weeks mixed up. But that couldn't be. If that were the case, then where had Mei Lai been that first week?

'I've just been told some rigmarole about her grandmother's condition deteriorating,' Tyler brought out, clearly unconcerned by anyone or anything but that his own arrangements should not be upset.

Laurie's lips tightened at his attitude, and she felt sorry herself to hear that her friend's grandmother was slipping away. And then as her brain raced, she thought she had a very good idea of how this whole mess had come about.

Mei Lai must have telephoned her employers from China asking for extra leave; granted in the compassionate circumstances of her grandmother being at death's door. In return for the favour her employers must have asked her if one of the buyers they wanted to keep in with from England could put up at her place. Mei Lai must have been so concerned about her grandmother, she had either forgotten she should already have two English visitors, or she had thought Laurie and Kay wouldn't mind sharing with another of their own countrymen. That must mean Mei Lai had a key to her flat at the office and that a representative from her firm had met Tyler at the airport and brought him on here. . . .

She left analysing the only explanation she could see as the terrible thought struck that even with Mei Lai there, Tyler's presence in the flat would be more than she could take—without her there, it would be impossible.

'You'll have to go to a hotel,' she told him, not having to think about it. He would be on expenses, he could afford it better than she could.

'Like hell I'll go to a hotel,' he came back, clearly not liking having his decisions made for him. 'I hate hotels.'

'You stayed in a hotel in Peking.'

'I didn't have any choice,' he said tersely. And, laying it on the line, 'If anybody's moving out, Miss Frost, it's you.'

'If anybody . . .?' she flared, hating him suddenly, not bothering to wonder where her love had gone. 'You know as well as I do there's only one bedroom.'

'I'm not sleeping on that miniature settee,' he told her adamantly.

Furious that he looked unmovable on the subject, Laurie searched in her bag for her case key. The swine! There wasn't one gentlemanly instinct in him. To think she had been ready to crumble when in that park he had said 'Poor little love'! God, they said love was blind. How right they were!

'Unpacking?' came the sarcastic query as she bent to unlock her case. 'You've decided to stay and make the best of it?'

Fury threatened to boil over at his sarcastic tone. She managed to conquer it. 'To use your expression,' she threw at him, 'like hell!'

Spitting mad, she flung back the lid of her case. Because of him, because of his steadfast refusal to move out, she was going to have to use what money she had left to pay a hotel bill. She'd have to change all her traveller's cheques too to pay for her accommodation, when she had been hoping to take maybe one of them back home to bolster up her ailing bank account.

She moved everything from the right-hand corner of her case, knowing she would find her wallet at the bottom. It wasn't there. It must have slipped while being tossed from one luggage handler to another, she thought, having been on two flights since she had last seen it. But search as she might, she still couldn't find it.

Damn, she'd have to take everything out of her case piece by piece, with him looking on too. 'Can't you go and find something to do?' she snapped, several pairs of lacy briefs in her hand.

'If your intention is to re-pack your case more tidily, you're not making much of a job of it,' came the cool reply behind her.

'I'm looking for something,' she said hotly, then forgot him, as although everything was now out of her case she still hadn't come across her wallet.

Still not ready to believe it wasn't there, she shook every article out as everything on the floor beside her was folded and put back in, her face paling when, the last item folded, she just had to believe it.

'It's not there!' she whispered, stunned, her anger with Tyler gone.

'Not to worry,' he said, entirely unmoved that she seemed to have some crisis on her hands, 'With your *assets*, no doubt you can soon buy another.'

'It's my wallet,' she said, groping for a chair, too upset to flare up at the insolent way he was suggesting she used what attributes she had. 'It's missing!'

'Missing?' Laurie didn't award him any marks that at last she was getting through. 'Are you sure?'

'Of course I'm sure. I've just had everything out of my case, haven't I?'

'Did you put it in your case? I seem to remember you had a wallet in your hand when we were changing our Chinese currency in Canton,' he pointed out reasonably.

'I have two wallets,' she explained, starting to get snappy again, not seeing anything he said as being reasonable, she was so upset. 'I thought with all the different currency I'd be using floating about I'd be bound to get mixed up.' And more to herself as she went through what she had done, 'My handbag started to get weighed down with all the various things I'd collected, so I put my Hong Kong wallet at the bottom of my case, meaning to take it out this morning.'

'Only you forgot.'

There he went again, making her feel stupid! 'There wasn't time to remember everything,' she said flatly.

'When did you use it last?' he asked, causing some of the chill she felt towards him to leave now he was sounding as though he wanted to help her.

'At the hotel in Peking, that first morning we were

there,' she remembered without any trouble. 'I needed to change a traveller's cheque . . .'

'Your traveller's cheques were in it!' he exclaimed, as though it was the daftest thing he had heard yet, that she hadn't kept them separate.

Her lips firmed. 'Yes,' she muttered.

There followed a silence where she wouldn't look at him. 'You're sure you didn't drop it in the hotel?' he asked quietly into the silence.

'I've just told you,' she said, trying not to get angry, 'I remember putting it in my case. I did it the night I'd bought a guide book and a map I thought it might be useful to carry around with me.' She didn't add in case she got lost, he would know that without her having to say so.

'And your case has been through God knows how many hands since then,' Tyler said slowly. Then, seriously looking for ways to help her, 'Have you your cheque book and bank card with you? If your bank has a branch here you can change a cheque for . . .'

'I didn't bring it,' she said woodenly. Fat lot of good bringing it would have done; her account was cleared out. Before she had lost her traveller's cheques she had known she would have to scrape along until her next salary cheque was paid in.

'You changed your yuan for Hong Kong dollars, didn't you?' Tyler asked, having witnessed that much at the airport. 'How much have you got?'

'Just over fifty dollars,' she said, wishing she hadn't been so liberal with her tip to the cabby. 'That wouldn't pay for a bed in a hotel for one night, let alone the next five,' she added, wondering if he did have a human streak after all and would under the circumstances offer to go.

'What you need is a cup of tea,' he said, turning to the kitchen, either not seeing her massive hint, or quite obviously ignoring it.

Laurie supposed it was kind of him to make her a cup of tea, she thought, trying to be fair some ten minutes later when he joined her at the table, two cups of tea adorning it.

In silence she stared at the brew in front of her. To his credit Tyler was silent too, giving her this time to sort herself out as she wondered where she went from here. Home was the only answer. But she didn't want to go home. She had beggared herself to pay for this trip. She wanted to get everything out of it she could. Both she and Kay had cut out cinemas, theatres, cut down on every expense they could. Why should she go home just because some light-fingered pest to society had stolen her money?

Aggression against the thief rose in her. She'd be dammed if she would let it ruin her holiday! Her eyes slid to the settee, measuring it for her length, and she stifled a sigh. Being a bit over five foot six she'd be a mass of creaks from just one night spent on it. Yet she still didn't see why Tyler shouldn't try it.

She looked at him, about to suggest it again, then she saw he had read her mind as slowly his head went from side to side in an unspoken negative reply.

'You can have the bottom bunk if you like,' he offered, that alone telling her he still had no intention of going to a hotel.

'Thanks for nothing, Mr Gray,' she said shortly, noting his surprised look that she knew his name. 'I'd die sooner than share a room with you!'

'You'll have to let me know what flowers you like,' he retorted pleasantly, just as though from his angle he couldn't see she had any other choice.

Throwing him a look of loathing, Laurie stood up, grabbed up her handbag, grappled against the urge to clout him with it, and went out.

The cocky devil! He knew it all, didn't he? she fumed, a picture of Mei Lai's settee in her mind. She had found it comfortable enough to sit on, but its hard arms either end, and the four feet or so in between, were just not in any way calculated to ensure restful slumber.

Laurie mooched around the various markets—fish stalls with no fish known to her on display, open-fronted shops from which exuded all manner of smells. She sneezed a couple of times, lost in the maze of different things for sale, and walked on, seeing the knife sharpener she had seen before busy at work with his honing stone on the pavement, a cobbler likewise in his shanty covering labouring away at his last.

And unbelievably in the circumstances, after about an hour of walking, of market stall and window shopping, that same inner feeling of happiness that must be common only to Hong Kong, she thought, was there again.

She didn't understand it. Everything that could possibly go wrong had gone wrong, not least her arrangements with Mei Lai falling apart—and Tyler Gray was king of the castle. But it was back again, that inner feeling of joy.

And she was glad it was. Her despairing spirits had lifted. It wasn't just that she was away from Tyler and his sarcastic tongue, she felt certain. It must be something peculiar to this colony, that no matter what trauma one suffered, it didn't get one down for long.

Feeling hot, parched for a drink of some sort, she found a small park and sat resting, the small fountain playing torture to her thirst. She mustn't give in and go and buy a glass of squash, she thought, her very limited resources to the forefront of her mind.

She sat in the park for an age, the traffic of Hong Kong still heard but not seen. But at the end of that time, several conclusions had been forced upon her. One, that for tonight at least she was going to have to spend a very uncomfortable night on that settee, two, that tomorrow she would have to get to the airport and see what she could do about changing her flight. Too late now. The airport was in Kowloon. There would probably be airport tax to pay and she couldn't risk her precious resources on a taxi. She would start out early tomorrow on foot, cross on the ferry to Kowloon—that was only thirty cents— then by Shanks's pony again to the airport. It would be hard going carrying her case—her mind refused to consider what she was going to do if she couldn't get a flight out the next day.

With everything sorted out in her mind, aware she was starving and hopeful that Tyler Gray hadn't hogged the few tinned supplies Mei Lai had in her tiny cupboard beneath her even tinier fridge in the kitchen, Laurie rose ready for the walk back.

It was then, as she passed the man who had been sitting some seats away reading a newspaper for some time, that she realised in the fading light that unless he had got X-ray vision, he could not possibly see to read. She looked back—she had to; and fear had her by the throat. It was the man she had thought was following her!

Trying not to panic, she hurried out of the park clutching her handbag under her arm, the fingers of her other hand tight on its strap in case she should be caught unawares and that man tried to grab it from her. He must be after that ring, he must be, she thought, diving in and out of traffic, her eyes searching frantically for a policeman with the red flash beneath his number that signified he could speak English.

She didn't see any sign of a policeman. Not that she was sure what she would have said to one anyway, she thought, as she sped on, getting over her initial panic.

And by the time she did espy a navy-uniformed officer of the law, she had gone off the idea of appealing to him. What could he do? She was sure the man following her would slip out of sight the minute she approached the officer.

Still expecting to have her handbag wrenched from her

grasp, or worse, be mugged from behind, she was never more grateful, her breath coming in painful gasps, to see the building where Mei Lai had her apartment.

She couldn't wait for the lift, but went as fast as she could up the three flights of stairs, some subconscious thought telling her she would be safe only when she reached Tyler.

Not wanting to let go her tight hold on her bag, even though she could not hear footsteps coming from behind, Laurie rang the bell, and stood there panting and anxious in the seconds it took for Tyler to answer it.

'Forget your key?' he enquired as he slid back the gate.

But she had no mind to heed his sarcasm. She was inside like a flash, all but collapsing into a seat. For her race home had been all of two miles. She heard the door close, felt a glass of something pushed into her hand, that in itself indicating that Tyler had seen her distressed condition, before he asked quietly:

'What is it?'

'Someone—was—following me.'

There was a pause before he spoke. 'Take a sip of that,' he urged. Then taking the chair opposite as she gulped from the glass, finding it was nothing more innocuous than water, 'You're sure about this, Laurie?'

She nodded. 'Positive,' she gasped.

'What did he look like? Was he Chinese?'

'No—European. Tall, bald head—moustache.' Tyler was at the door before she had any idea what he was about. 'Don't—leave me,' she cried, and was in love with him all over again when he gave her that gentle smile.

'I won't be long,' he promised. 'Check through the spy-hole before you open the door.'

He had gone before it dawned on her what he meant. Mei Lai's door, like all flat doors in Hong Kong, she suspected, had a marble-sized piece of magnified glass set in it.

Her breathing was more normal by the time she heard Tyler come back. But she was still upset enough to need to peer through the marble pebble before she let him in.

'He wasn't there, was he?' she asked anxiously.

'I had a good scout round,' he assured her.

'I didn't imagine he was following me, honestly I didn't. It isn't the first time I've been followed either.'

'I don't suppose it is,' said Tyler easily, an unexpected compliment there to her looks if she had been in a mind to appreciate it.

'It isn't,' she insisted. 'He was at the airport today. And ... and I saw him watching me before I went to China.'

'But you didn't see him in China?' His very tone told her he was begining to be sceptical that she had seen anybody at all.

'No,' she had to admit, and was disappointed in him. He had seemed to believe her when she had first come in, but now he had been outside and not found her sleuth, he was treating the whole matter far too lightly, in her view. 'You don't believe me, I know you don't. But I *was* being followed,' she said stubbornly. 'And not because of what you were implying just now either.'

'I haven't said I don't believe you, have I?' he asked. 'But accepting that it wasn't some young blood who'd been bowled over by your beauty,' he said it without making it sound a compliment, as though her beauty was a fact, but this time Laurie did feel complimented by his comment, 'what reason,' he pressed, 'could your bald-headed friend have for following you?'

The glow from his unintended compliment faded. He knew, damn him, he knew! He knew very well about that ring in her bag! She remembered his barking, 'Where the *hell* did you get that?'—his remarks that had followed, and she knew just then, her fright having taken

the stuffing out of her, that she wasn't up to dealing
with any more of the same.

'How should I know?' she said, playing the same game
as him. And getting up from her chair she went and sat
on the settee, presenting him with her profile, letting him
see that as far as she was concerned the subject was now
finished with.

Laurie started to feel better once she was away from
where she could see his disbelieving face. She began to
recover from her fright. She felt safe in Mei Lai's flat
away from any fears, real or imaginary, that she might be
mugged at any moment. Though she hadn't imagined it,
she was sure she hadn't, she thought, growing mutinous
that Tyler, clattering away in the kitchen, had considered
the subject finished with too, since he had not commented
after she had removed herself from the table to the settee.

Not another word had he said, she mused, half ready to
be angry with him. The next thing she had heard was
him in the kitchen.

Her stomach was letting her know she was ravenous,
and she wished he would hurry up with whatever he was
doing in there so she could find something to eat. The
kitchen was so small there just wasn't room enough for
two in there.

Smells of something deliciously appetising wafted her
way, making it sheer torture to sit there contemplating
the small tin of baked beans she would have to eat without
bread—her one hope was that Tyler hadn't helped himself
to them.

'Feel like laying the table?'

She slewed round and saw him filling the kitchen doorway. Lay it yourself, she wanted to say, mutiny with her
that he was going to have a feast, by the smell of it, while
all she had was a plate of baked beans. Then she was glad
she managed to hold her tongue, even though the way
she glared at him wasn't missed, she was sure, when a

slow smile creased his face.

'I have the most succulent steak you've ever seen about ready to serve,' he tormented. And when, if she had anything handy she was sure she would have thrown it at his mocking face, he added, 'But alas, I fear there's too much for one.' Her juices were already at work. 'Will you help me out?'

'Er—if you insist,' she said, trying to sound cool.

But she couldn't keep it up. She was happy suddenly. She smiled, a natural smile that wouldn't stay down, and saw his eyes on her mouth, before abruptly he turned back into the kitchen.

He had been right about the steak being succulent, she thought some fifteen minutes later, as she popped the last piece into her mouth.

'You went shopping after I left?' she queried, when he pushed a plate of cheese and biscuits her way.

'Not all males are helpless when it come to that sort of thing,' he answered, sending the thought rushing through her head that in normal circumstances she would like to bet he got his girl-friends to do his shopping.

'So you've proved,' she replied, forcing a smile because she didn't want him to know how sick she felt that he would never ask her to shop for him, never count her as a girl-friend.

His look became fixed on her smile, her lips, then abruptly he took his eyes from her and stood up, his look going to the kitchen. Laurie was sure she felt tension in the air, but there was none there when Tyler directed his look back on her.

'There's a mountain of washing up in there,' he said, resignation in his voice.

'I'll do it,' she offered instantly, the least she could do since he had fed her so well.

'There's only room for one in there,' Tyler added, the smirk on his face telling her that while he didn't mind cooking, dealing with dirty pans afterwards wasn't his idea of fun.

'Clever devil,' she said goodhumouredly, seeing as she rose and began to collect up the dishes that that resigned note in his voice had been there deliberately to get her to volunteer.

He was sitting on the settee reading, his back to her, when with a feeling of general tiredness about her, Laurie came out of the kitchen. He turned his head to glance her way when she sat down at the table.

'You looked whacked,' he remarked. 'Why not go to bed?'

He wants me out of his sight, she thought, love for him making her overly sensitive where he was concerned. He wants to read his book, and my presence in the same room is irritating him.

Her, 'I'll go when you go,' came out more snappily than she intended. But when she saw the way his dark eyebrows rose at her choice of words, she was glad she had snapped, and snapped again as she told him heatedly, 'And you can forget any quaint ideas you may have from what I've just said. I'm sleeping out here, not in there.' Her eyes indicated the bedroom, as she accused, 'You're sitting on my bed!'

She had drawn his anger, she could see that as his brow came down. His paperback was flung from his hands as he stood to his feet and gave her one killing look before striding to the bedroom. In seconds he had returned, his arms full of the duvet he had snatched up from one of the bunks.

He threw it to the settee, his expression none the sweeter as he glowered at her. 'For your information, Miss Frost, you'll be as undisturbed in this flat as if you were in a nunnery. Should the idea of bedding you have crossed my mind at any time, then count on it, any such notion disappeared way back at the airport in Canton.'

She had just time enough to get in one furious burst before he returned to the bedroom and the door thundered home. 'That's just as well,' she stormed. 'You had as much chance then as you have now!'

Unmitigated swine! she fumed as she searched in her case for her night things. Should the idea of bedding her have crossed his mind? It dammed well had! For ten minutes she crashed about, washing, cleaning her teeth in the minute bathroom next to the bedroom.

It was that perishing ring, of course, she fumed as she tossed this way and that trying to find a position of comfort on the settee. He had lost interest in her from the moment he had seen it and recognised it for the very expensive item it was, had dubbed her straight away as a girl who gave nothing for nothing. Not that she cared,—the caustic, ill-tempered oaf!

That was probably why he hadn't offered to lend her any money to tide her over when he knew she was as good as flat broke, she thought, adjusting her position once more. Not that she would have taken it anyway. But she hadn't had the chance to refuse. Believing he could say goodbye to any money he lent her, he hadn't even offered.

Two hours later she was still trying to sleep and hating Tyler Gray more than ever that he was probably snoring his head off in there. Her thoughts had been many and varied as she tried to shut out the racket that went on constantly through the night outside. She had forgotten all about the din from goods being loaded and unloaded while the constant tapping of metal upon metal, a technique used in China, to guide reversing lorries.

Lord, she was tired! Would she never get to sleep? He might have tossed a pillow out as well as the duvet, she thought crossly, the hard arm was giving her neck-ache.

Had Mei Lai, if things had gone as planned, intended one of them to sleep on this insomniac-making settee? she couldn't help wondering. There would have been three of them if Kay's appendix hadn't erupted and Mei Lai hadn't had to stay by her grandmother's bedside.

Perhaps she had been going to borrow a camp bed from somewhere, Laurie thought, yawning, but nowhere nearer to going to sleep. Oh hell, this was impossible!

In the middle of thanking goodness she had already purchased all the presents to take home, so no one need be disappointed since she didn't have the wherewithal to buy anything else, not that anyone was expecting anything—her mother had said specifically not to bring her anything—Laurie turned over again, and fell off the settee.

She perched back on the settee, clutching the duvet around her bare arms, and pondered.

Would Rip Van Winkle in there have snaffled the bottom bunk? This was too ridiculous for words! She remembered how comfortable she had been in bed that first week, how soon forgotten were the outside noises, how soon she had fallen asleep and slept undisturbed by the racket until morning.

If Tyler had taken the bottom bunk she didn't reckon much to her chances of shinning up to the top without waking him and so losing face. But—but if he had taken the top bunk then surely she could sneak in for a few hours' sleep? She always awoke at first light before she drifted off again.

The idea, born in desperation, wouldn't go away. She was confident of her early waking pattern, wasn't she? Even in her subconscious mindful of Tyler, when she woke at daybreak all she had to do was to sneak out again, and he would be none the wiser.

Tiptoeing over the polished wooden floor, the duvet held securely, Laurie felt for the door handle. The seconds it took her to open it seemed like minutes, so slowly did she turn it. She peered in the dim light, trying to make out if there was a shape on the bottom bunk.

She stretched down a hand, ready to stifle a scream if she touched some solid object—and it moved. There was nothing there!

Afraid to close the door, not much point anyway since she would have to stealthily open it again when she made her dawn exit, she edged her body into the bunk.

She lay down, pulling the duvet over her, turned, heard the bunk creak and held her breath—but heard no sound of movement from up above but Tyler's even breathing.

She stretched out her long legs. Bliss, sheer unadulterated bliss, she thought, almost purring. Laurie closed her eyes.

CHAPTER SEVEN

A NOISE. Something had disturbed her! Lying on her side, Laurie opened her eyes, then quickly closed them. A pair of fawn trouser-clad legs were close to her bunk. *It was broad daylight out there!* What had happened to her built-in alarm clock? She *never* slept straight through—never. Had she been so tired from her day, that two-mile dash home— and it must have been gone two before she had crept into bed—that she had gone out like a light, her usual dawn awaking slept through?

'There's tea made,' said a cool sardonic voice, his tone telling her not only that he knew she was awake, but also that he had never believed in her stout intention not to share a room with him.

Laurie waited for a sound that would tell her he had gone before she opened her eyes a second time. The trousered legs weren't there, she saw, and gathered he must have found whatever he had come in for.

His offer of tea appealed. She threw back the duvet, put her feet to the floor and was standing in her flimsy cotton nightie having a lovely stretch before she noticed he had left the bedroom door wide and wasn't above appreciating her curves outlined through the thin cotton, for all he had said he had gone off any idea he might have had of bedding her.

A spurt of temper had her slamming the door shut with a crash. Then she found herself in something of a dilemma. All her clothes were out there! Oh, why hadn't she thought to bring in her dressing gown? Because you anticipated being out of here before he awoke, came the answer.

About to grab up the duvet to see her through till she could get in there to put on her robe, her movement was stayed by the door opening.

'I thought in the circumstances your modesty would forgive my sorting through your case,' said Tyler, as mockingly he handed her her dressing gown.

She took it from him, her eyes daggers in his back as he went. Then as she hastily wrapped herself in the garment she saw he wasn't all bad, for he wasn't pouring himself two separate cups of tea, was he?

He was sitting at the table when she went in, a faint smell of aftershave clinging to him. Laurie afforded him a quick lift at the corners of her mouth in what would do as a half smile as she went to sit down, then wished she had kept her face unsmiling when he ordered:

'Put something on your feet.'

'I prefer to go around barefoot,' she said, knowing he brought out the worst in her, that she was just being difficult because she didn't like any man thinking he could boss her around.

'Suit yourself,' he answered laconically. 'But don't come screaming to me if a cockroach comes nibbling at your pretty toes.'

Memory returned of seeing more than one cockroach since she had been in Hong Kong, and the perversity in her died as she got up and rooted by the settee for her slippers.

She expected Tyler to look smug that she had given in without a fight. That he wasn't looking smug when she flicked a glance at him, though, didn't help at all when she was still feeling vexed that he had discovered her will power was puny when up against a settee that overnight seemed to be stuffed with rocks and the comfort of that bunk bed.

'And what do you plan to do today?' he enquired as she sipped her tea.

Why should he think he owned the sole rights to sarcasm? 'I thought I'd go and book in at the Peninsula,' she said airily, mentioning off the top of her head the most expensive-looking hotel she could remember seeing. Then she found her sarcasm just wasn't in the same league as he made her blood boil with his sharp retort:

'I don't doubt you'd soon find some poor sap to foot the bill.'

Red flashed before her eyes at his low opinion of her. She was on her feet, the cup in her hand flying, hot tea going in a line for him. It would have hit him too had he not moved quickly—so quickly that he was on his feet and had her by the wrists, his face furious as he hauled her up against him.

Laurie's heart hammered beneath her thin clothing as his head, showing aggression, came nearer, her temper vanishing as rapidly as it had come. She wanted to tell him she was sorry—but that need was only of a short duration. More than wanting to apologise, the feel of him close to her had her wanting to feel his lips on hers, wanted them to burn as they had done before, as his body was burning hers.

Her lips parted as his mouth neared. Then suddenly, when nothing mattered but that he should kiss her, Tyler was thrusting her away, had released the grip he had on her, and was gritting through clenched teeth:

'Go and get dressed—not all men desire to take what's on offer.'

Stunned, unable to come so quickly back down to earth, for several seconds she just stood and stared at him, the hurt showing in her eyes. Then fury returned to help her out. Only this time she had to control it. Moving swiftly, she grabbed the clothes she needed from her case, stepped over the line of tea on the floor—let him clean it up, damn him!—and was in the bathroom, the door slammed and bolted.

Under the shower she was nowhere near to cooling off. If she said another word to him it would be to tell him to get lost, she boiled. The shower too came in for some of her anger in that it wouldn't behave and kept moving loosely about. Her hair was getting soaked, but since she was in no hurry to rejoin that—that barbarian, she found shampoo in her toilet bag and washed it—to remember only as she turned off the shower and began to dry off that if she was going to go to the airport, it would have to be with a wet head.

The tea had been cleaned from the floor when she came out of the bathroom clad in a tee-shirt and jeans. A feeling of guilt she didn't want smote her that she should have been the one to clear it up—that in itself told her her anger had cooled.

'You don't look as though you intend going anywhere for a while.' It surprised her to hear his voice sounding quite amiable. After the fury that had been in the air not half an hour ago she had thought he wouldn't want to speak to her either. 'Unless of course your friend has a hairdryer tucked away somewhere,' he added, seeming to know her thick hair would take hours to dry without an aid of some sort.

'I'm not in the habit of raking through other people's belongings,' she said primly, breaking her vow of silence where he was concerned.

She saw him raise an eyebrow and counselled herself not to get angry again that he hadn't credited her with any honesty.

'Well, I'm off,' he said. And grudgingly, Laurie found herself liking him again, for when had he not moved quickly she would have scalded him with her tea, it appeared he had been waiting for her to come from the bathroom to see if she wanted anything while he was out. 'I should be back before lunch—anything you need?'

'No, thank you,' she replied, too proud to accept his

charity, though admitting his offer had mellowed her. He was at the door before the feel of wet hair in her neck had her asking, 'Er—you're not by any chance going near the airport, are you?'

'Airport?' he queried, then coming away from the door, his eyes narrowed. 'I might be—why?'

'I was going to see if I could change my ticket, get a flight home today.'

'You're ready to go home?'

The surprise in his voice had her surprised in return. Why should it surprise him that she should want to go home? He knew her circumstances as well as she did. She saw speculation in his eyes—it was as though, she thought, trying to understand it, as though he thought she was up to something. He confirmed it.

'Just what sort of a game are you playing?' he asked, his voice harsh.

'What the hell does that mean?' she asked hotly, her temper rearing again. 'What game? You know damn well that I'm broke—I can't even feed myself—where would I go but home?'

'All right, don't blow a fuse.' His own manner had quickly changed as he set about soothing her ruffled feathers. 'My God, what a hothead you are! Just cool down and give me your ticket.' His look became mocking. 'It will be a pleasure to try and change it for you.'

He seemed to delight in trying to get a rise out of her, she thought after he had gone. And where on earth had her control of her temper gone? Did everybody go haywire like this when they fell in love? Ready to take offence at the smallest slight? Not that his slights had been small. Never had she been so insulted by a man. Yet—yet still she loved him.

Knowing such thoughts were going to get her nowhere, Laurie set about tidying up the small flat. She hadn't had breakfast, neither had Tyler. Perhaps like her he was never hungry in the mornings. Oh, stop thinking about him!

Next she set about tidying her case. She didn't want it looking like a junk shop if Customs wanted to see inside at Gatwick. She came across a spare postcard in the process and decided to scribble a few lines to Kay. She'd probably see her before she received it, she thought, be back in England anyway. Still, if Kay was confined to her flat during her convalescence, then it was always nice to have the postman call.

She felt better after she had penned a cheery message to her friend, and in consequence was much brighter when she heard Tyler's key in the gate.

She looked at him eagerly when he came in, then had to lower her eyes as just seeing him, those dark eyes, that thick black hair, started a riot going on inside her. Her eyes were drawn to him again when without a word he bent to move her case out of his way from where she had left it by the door.

Her eyes followed him, a mixture of emotions besetting her that he didn't want her luggage cluttering up the living area in any way. She watched as he took her case to the bedroom, saw in view of the limited space, the way he stacked it upright on top of his upright case by the far wall.

Impatient to hear about her flight, ready to be on her way as soon as he said what time, her eyes asked the question as soon as he returned.

'No go, I'm afraid,' he said, trying not to look as regretful as she was sure he felt. 'I tried all the airlines, but every one of them is booked solid.'

She knew he was speaking the truth. The fact that he had tried every airline underlined how keen he was to get rid of her. But even so she just couldn't take in that she was stranded here, virtually penniless.

'But—but there were loads of empty seats on the plane coming out!'

'I know,' he commiserated. 'It was the same on my flight too.'

Laurie sighed, wondering how long it was possible for the human frame to go without food. Tyler heard her sigh and took pity on her, which was something she just did not want.

'Your hair looks about dry now. Come on, I'll take you to lunch.'

'No, thank you, I'm not hungry,' she lied, starving now where she hadn't been before. Then she heard him say, his voice quiet, gentle almost:

'Don't be stubborn, Laurie.'

Tears pricked her eyes at his tone. How easily he could get to her by being kind, whereas when he was angry, he just drew sparks. She lowered her eyes, not wanting him to see she was ready to flood the place at any crumb of kindness from him.

'I don't want charity,' she mumbled.

'Don't look on it as charity,' he said in that same quiet way. 'You're stuck here until next Thursday. It's only Saturday now—you've got to eat. We're the same nationality and you'd do the same for me, wouldn't you?' Laurie didn't answer. 'Or would you?' he asked, a teasing note there.

'Yes, I suppose so,' she answered, and had to smile at him when he tilted her head up and she saw he was smiling.

'There you are, then,' he said. 'Now come on, there's a good girl, my stomach's sticking to my backbone.'

He'd scuppered her, charmed her, had her barely capable of thinking. So much so that it was he who saw the card she had written lying on the table and picked it up to take with them.

Her pride surfaced as they walked along the pavements, pride in being with him. They were the only Westerners in the district, but it wasn't just that that made people

look at him, she thought, Tyler would be noticed everywhere he went.

They were passing a post office she hadn't recognised
as such, when Tyler said he'd nip in and post her card for
her. 'I can do it,' she protested.

'Stay here and wait for me,' he instructed, and was
inside before she could stop him.

About to follow him, pride decreeing she paid the postage herself, she checked. They hadn't fired up at each
other once since he had come back. Was it worth having
a free-for-all inside the post office, all on account of a
stamp? Besides which, Tyler had his pride too. Wouldn't
he be offended if in front of everyone in there she made it
look as if he was hard up for the postage too by insisting
she paid?

She looked about her and remembered the bald-headed
man from yesterday, and was suddenly nervous. Oh,
where was Tyler? she thought, agitatedly clutching on to
her bag; she felt safe with him.

He touched her arm and she jumped. 'Oh!' she exclaimed.

'You're pale. What's the matter?'

Nothing now he was back. 'I—I just thought about the
man who followed me yesterday. I . . .'

'You thought he might be following you again today?'
She didn't answer. He hadn't believed there had been
any bald-headed man anyway. 'I'm sure you won't see
him again,' he told her, making her feel better already
that maybe he did believe her. 'But just in case, you'd
better stick close to me.'

He took her to the City Hall for lunch. And in the cool
brown and white surroundings, sipping a refreshing glass
of water brought to each of them as they waited for their
meal, Laurie began to relax.

'You're looking better,' Tyler commented as their first
course was brought. 'Feeling more like the Lauretta who

had a temper to match her hair?'

'I'm sorry I nearly threw my tea over you,' she said quietly, the apology long overdue.

He didn't say, you would have been had it reached its target, but it was there briefly in his eyes. Laurie looked away and began to tuck in, glad he hadn't said what was clearly in his mind. Perhaps he too was being on his best behaviour, she mused. Maybe he too had decided to guard his tongue and not say anything that would have her flaring in retaliation. At any rate the meal progressed without aggravation coming from either side, nothing but pleasantness coming from Tyler, so that by the time they reached the dessert stage, Laurie was feeling quite enchanted.

Music was coming from a tape somewhere, soft and soothing. When she heard the strains of *Stranger In Paradise* it was so exactly as she felt. She raised her eyes and saw, her breath catching, that Tyler was looking at her as though there was that same enchantment in the air for him too.

She smiled, simply because she could do no other, and thought he was going to smile back, then came down to earth with a bump.

'If you've finished your pudding,' he said shortly, his eyes going from her to her dessert plate, 'I'll take you up the Peak.'

Enchantment was shattered—was shattered by him. And remembering some of the vile things he had said to her, she was glad. She had been in cloud cuckoo land there for a while. Nothing had been said of when he was returning to England, but if he was staying at Mei Lai's flat for the same length of time as she was, those long nights to be got through, then she had to keep to the forefront of her mind that whatever brief impulses came to him from time to time, she would do well to remember that when it came down to basics, he had lost interest in her at that airport in Canton.

The cable car ride up to the Peak was so steep it kept her back glued to her seat. But the view over Hong Kong and across the harbour to Kowloon was magnificent. A fine mist hung in the air, but it was so warm she was glad she hadn't brought a jacket. She concentrated on the view, not having anything to say to Tyler who since they had left City Hall had been silent to the point of being morose.

It seemed farcical to be with him now his manner had changed. She could just have easily walked back home, she mused, pretending the view had her whole attention and that she wasn't aware of him by her side. She would have suggested going back too had she not thought that would have them involved in further verbal fisti-cuffs.

The thought came, and wouldn't depart, that perhaps he would have been glad if she had suggested they part company, and colour came to her face that he might be an unwilling escort. She waited for her colour to recede, then turned, intending to tell him she was going home.

'You forgot your camera,' he said, before she could get in first, his tone teasing, unbelievably no longer the morose man he had been. And more unbelievably still, 'This is one of the few times I wish I carried a camera around with me.' And while Laurie was still trying to adjust to the sudden change in him, he was all charm as he said, 'I'd like to take a shot of you as you are now, the sun catching your newly washed hair, the wind teasing it. What a delightful picture that would make!'

Staggered, for surely he must be complimenting her, Laurie forgot what she had been going to say, if she had been going to say anything.

'I'll bet you say that to all the girls,' was the best she could manage.

'Only on Fridays,' he answered.

'This is Saturday,' she reminded him.

'Then, my dear Laurie,' he said softly, 'you must be unique.'

She looked away, intent on the view again, treachery at work in her heart against the good sense in her head. Her heart chose that moment to goad her into wanting to explain to Tyler about that ring, to let him know that whatever black thoughts he had about her, and he must have had some of those as they had finished their meal, then those black thoughts had no foundation.

Steady, ruled her head. Wasn't it better to put up with his change of mood whenever something triggered off a reminder of the sort of person he thought she was? Wasn't it better that the nicer side of him, that side that had her wilting, should not be permanently on display?

If she told him the innocent story of the ring might he not return to the person who in China had made no bones about the attraction that was there for them both? He had been ready for a holiday romance then. Might he not attempt to kiss her again if she told him? Could she resist his kisses? Would she have the strength to resist him at all—when all he wanted was a few nights of pleasure, and then goodbye, So long, Laurie, nice knowing you?

She kept the truth of the ring to herself, but made her manner carefully friendly as they turned and went the way they had come. But it was hard work for her to keep from telling him. It had her searching in her mind for some subject that had nothing to do with either of them in her endeavours to keep things impersonal between them.

'I noticed that tree with the beautiful pale pinky mauve flower growing in several avenues in Canton,' she said, pointing to a beautiful blossoming tree, and wishing she hadn't reminded him of Canton.

'The Hong Kong Orchid Tree,' he filled in for her, the mocking look he gave her giving her an idea that he knew

she wasn't entirely at ease with him. She was sure of it
when he gave her chapter and verse on the tree. 'It has
been adopted as Hong Kong's floral emblem. It was discovered in the Pokfulam area of Hong Kong in 1908 and
named *Bauhinia Blakeiana* after Sir Henry Blake, a former
governor.'

'Are you airing your knowledge or just delighting in
sending me up?' she challenged him huffily.

'I thought you were interested in such things,' he
replied innocently—butter wouldn't melt. 'I thought you
would never see enough of that red and green-leafed tree
in Canton.'

She *was* interested in such things. Any growing thing
caught her attention. But having been at pains to keep
everything between them impersonal, Laurie found to her
confusion that she didn't want that either.

'Stop looking sulky and come and have a cup of tea,'
he said, which didn't help matters.

'Damn you, Tyler Gray!' she suddenly flared. 'Go and
have tea by yourself—I'm fed up with your charity!'

'And I'm fed up with you,' he bit, as aggressive as her,
and with the same promptitude. 'You're never the same
two minutes together.'

'*I'm* never the same!'

'We did the charity bit back at the flat,' he grated. 'So
damn well forget it. It bores me.'

About to flare again, nobody had ever accused her of
being boring before, Laurie counted ten and swallowed a
huge chunk of pride.

'Thank you for your offer of tea,' she said woodenly,
'but I'm not thirsty.'

'I've gone off the idea myself,' Tyler told her coldly.
Then, obviously making the same effort she was making,
'If it's not beneath your dignity, you can come and guide
me round a supermarket.'

It rankled that he had said she looked sulky, but fairness

had her admitting, as they shopped half an hour later, that perhaps her bottom lip had jutted, only slightly, though. He had told her to help herself from the shelves to anything she fancied—which she wouldn't—and was doing his best to help her, she reasoned, with yet more fairness. It wasn't his fault that he had her behaving at times in a manner she didn't recognise as the Laurie Frost she had always been.

They were in a taxi heading back to the flat with their plastic carriers, when, sorely wanting to be friends again, she tried to get back to being the girl she had been before she had met him.

'Are you dining out tonight?' she asked.

'Are you angling for an invitation to come with me?' he replied coolly, just as though he didn't put it past her to ask any man to take her out.

Her pride pricked, her eyes stung. 'No, I'm not!' she snapped, then despaired of ever getting back to normal. She swallowed down tears. 'I merely thought, since there's enough food here to feed an army, that—that if you intended staying in for dinner, then—then I would cook it for you.'

She looked out of the car window, her vision blurred to the scene outside. Then she felt him take her hand in his, heard his voice, kind, like it had been before.

'It really hurts, doesn't it?' he said, and for a moment she knew fear that he had discovered her love for him. 'It hurts you to take something from me.'

Tears threatened to choke her, the kindness in his tone did nothing to help, and it was some moments before she could reply.

'You s-seem determined to see me as something I'm not.' she choked at last, nearer than ever to telling him about that ring.

'And what are you?' he asked softly.

His hand on hers was warm and sensitive, causing her

to have to swallow again before she spoke. 'I'm just a straightforward secretary trying to enjoy a straightforward three-week holiday. Only—only because I've lost my money, with no chance of getting a flight home before Thursday night, I'm forced to st-stay in a flat with a man for company who thinks I'm some—some . . .' Her voice petered out, not sure any more what Tyler thought she was.

But her bringing up the subject of what he thought of her had hardened something in him. That kindness in him was gone anyway when next she heard his voice.

His hand left hers. 'And you're not?' he asked roughly.

He had fired her anger, and the tears instantly dried that it didn't seem they could go five minutes without fighting. 'No, I'm not,' she said heatedly. It was that blessed ring, of course, but she'd be hanged if she'd tell him about it now.

'In that case,' said Tyler, after a few seconds pause, his voice mild in comparison with what it had been, 'you can show me what sort of a cook you are. But,' as he observed she had turned and was looking at him open-mouthed that he had so quickly changed again, 'only on condition you cook enough for two.'

CHAPTER EIGHT

LAURIE's habit of waking at dawn before snuggling down to finish her sleep out had returned by the time Wednesday came around. But that Wednesday morning she did not close her eyes and go back to sleep again. Instead she lay there listening to Tyler's rhythmic breathing in the bunk above and reflecting on the days they had spent together since she had cooked the evening meal on Saturday.

How marvellous each day had been! Tyler's moods were no longer so instantly changeable. Almost from the moment they had set foot in the flat again he had adopted an easy manner, a manner that had made it easier for her to go to bed that Saturday.

'I'm going to read for a while if you want to use the bathroom first,' he had suggested.

So she had. She had washed and changed into her night things, then bidden him a hasty goodnight and gone into the bedroom. And even though she thought she wouldn't, she had been asleep when he had come in.

It was as though he had called a truce, she mused. As though he had seen she was genuinely upset at taking his charity and had put aside his opinion of her in an endeavour to get her to make the best of it.

She lay there recalling how every morning he courteously asked if she had any plans for the day—taking a tough line with her yesterday, she remembered, the only sour note, when, because she had got round to thinking he must be getting tired of taking her about, she had independently said she had decided to wander about by herself that day.

'You've arranged to meet someone,' he had shot at her

sharply, making her think for one heady moment that she had seen jealousy there.

She turned away, hope vanishing. His attitude with her since Saturday had been so completely unsexual, nothing there to indicate that he thought of her in any way other than as a compatriot who was down on her luck. Not so much as a word out of place had he spoken. And since when she turned her head to look at him, and saw not an atom of jealousy in his face, only harshness that she was again spurning his charity as impatiently he waited for her answer, she knew with a dull feeling that when he had said he had gone off her in Canton, he had meant it.

'Who would I meet?' she asked reasonably enough, she'd thought. 'You're the only person I know here, aren't you?'

Tyler had turned away, his expression hostile still. And Laurie knew then that she could spend the day with the devil for all he cared. Then suddenly he was facing her, facing her as ruefully, and to her utmost joy he had said:

'I've rather got used to having you around—you're not going to deprive me of your company today, are you?'

Who wouldn't have given in when witnessing the coaxing smile that had accompanied his words? 'Well, if you put it like that.' She had been powerless to deny herself.

And although she knew he had long since shelved any notion of a holiday romance, yesterday had proved for her to be too blissful for words. They had taken a ferry to Lantau Island, and had visited a monastery there, Tyler's attitude remaining easy. But because she was once again at peace with him, bustling Hong Kong forgotten in that serene setting, she had been strangely at peace with herself. It had been a day to remember, she thought, drowsiness taking her, her eyes closing as she thought of that hairy drive up to the monastery.

'Are you getting up today?'

The sound of Tyler's voice on the other side of the door had her hastily swinging her feet over the side of her bunk, hating to lose a minute of her limited time with him—she would be flying home tomorrow night.

She was still tying her robe as she shot out of the door, then tried to sound casual, not let him see that just the sight of him had her heartbeats quickening.

'You rang sir?' she enquired.

'Slippers,' he reminded her, a grin coming her way.

Dutifully she complied. She had no intention of arguing with him in the time left.

'If you've nothing planned,' he said, pausing briefly to give her the chance to say what her plans were, continuing when she had not a word to say, 'I'll take you for a dim sum breakfast.'

Of all her experiences in Hong Kong, Laurie thought dim sum just had to be her favourite. Tyler took her to what must be the largest restaurant she had ever been in, but even so it was packed to capacity.

She waited while he went in search of a table, going with him when he came back and said they were in luck. Dim sum, he explained when they were seated, meant 'To touch the heart'.

That he held hers he must never know, she thought, as her eyes stared in fascination at all that was going on around her. The restaurant was filled with Chinese, families most of them, small children, some still in pyjamas. Trolleys holding steaming bamboo baskets being wheeled by every table, and their contents called out, the trolley pushers only stopping when the customer heard something called he fancied.

Not knowing the names of any of the dishes, Laurie had to leave it to Tyler to order for her. She was glad she had put in a little chopstick training in China as, sampling one dish after another, she ate spring rolls, which consisted of pork, spring onions and bean sprouts all deep fried in paper-thin pastry, then something called tsing ngau yuk which turned out to be beef ball in lotus leaf, and something called prawn cheung fun, which was a slippery roll of steamed rice batter with a prawn filling which she was sure Tyler had ordered to test her chopstick ability. She grinned at him unconcerned when the slippery object plopped back into her bowl, and grinned again—in gratitude—when he let go by a trolley containing braised chicken feet and duck feet.

All the while she had been sampling the different dishes, there had been a constant flow of two sorts of tea, jasmine and bo-li, the system being that as soon as one teapot was empty the teapot lid was taken and balanced on the pot and a keen-eyed waiter instantly came and refilled it.

Another trolley was paraded by. 'I'm full,' Laurie got in before another bamboo basket could be placed on the table.

'How about finishing with lin yung pau?' Tyler tempted. 'It's a sweet lotus paste inside a sweet steamed dumpling. I heard it called out over there, it won't be here for some minutes.'

'They work hard here, don't they?' Laurie said, giving in to the temptation of lin yung pau, and pouring Tyler another miniature cup of bo-li.

'Earn every cent, I would say,' he agreed.

That put her in mind to ask about his work. She knew he was a buyer here partly on business, but apart from that first morning when he had absented himself, he hadn't since done any work.

'Did you complete the business you came here to do?' she queried, interested in his work, but more hoping to learn when he was returning to England. Wouldn't it be too wonderful if he was on the same flight home as her?

'Not yet,' was his brief answer, giving her the idea that he didn't want to talk about his job.

'Who do you work for?' she followed up, ignoring her instincts that he didn't want to discuss his work in her need to find out more than the little he had allowed her to know before they parted. The look he gave her told her her instincts were right, made her feel slightly uncomfortable, for all it was such an everyday question. 'I just thought I might know them,' she tacked on lamely. 'The firm I work for have some dealings in electronics too.'

She felt better when after giving her a severe look, Tyler relented and told her the name of his employers. 'I work for a company in—Milton Keynes,' he told her, calling over the lady with the lin yung pau trolley. 'Bridge Electrics.'

'I've never heard of them,' said Laurie, helping herself from the bamboo basket.

'Do you know many firms in Milton Keynes?' he asked, expertly using his chopsticks on the latest dish.

'Well, no,' she replied with a smile, following up with, 'Have you worked for Bridge Electrics long?'

'More years than I can remember,' he teased her, and her smile broadened as she looked at him and wondered again how old he was. 'And in answer to your next question—I'm thirty-seven.'

'Thought-reader,' Laurie replied happily.

'And you are—twenty-two?'

'He guesses accurately as well,' she laughed.

'And how long have you worked for your present firm?' It was his turn to ask questions.

But whereas he had seemed disinclined to reveal anything about his work, Laurie had no such inhibitions. She wanted him to be interested in her, in what she did.

'Eighteen months,' she said, busy again with the teapot.

'You like your work?'

'Love it.'

'That tells me you get on well with your boss.'

'He's a sweetie,' said Laurie openly, and wondered why he frowned. Perhaps it was a trick of the light, she thought, for he wasn't frowning when next he spoke. But it was her turn to frown, for she didn't care at all for the implication behind what he said.

'I expect he chases you around the desk from time to time,' he remarked casually.

A chill she could do nothing about came over her. Did he think there was nothing she wouldn't do for promotion?

'Nothing like that goes on,' she said frigidly.

'You mean he carries a white stick?'

'He happens to be married.'

Tyler was definitely frowning, she saw, as he gritted, 'That makes a difference?'

The enjoyment she had found in her surroundings vanished, the marvellous atmosphere in the restaurant disappearing instantly. 'You never have believed I'm anything other than some hardhearted female with her eye to the main chance, have you?' she accused, growing too upset to want to stay there any more. She bent and picked up her bag from the floor. She was about to get to her feet when his hand came swiftly across the table to grip her wrist.

'You didn't earn that ring in your bag by being the sweet little darling you'd have me believe these last few days you are,' he said, his jaw showing an aggressive thrust. 'And don't tell me it has sentimental value, that you never go anywhere without it, because. . . .'

'It does have sentimental value,' she hissed at him.

'I'll bet it does,' he gritted, 'So much sentimental value you never wear it. The only sentiment about that ring as far as you're concerned is how much you'll get for it.'

'Get for it?'

'The only reason you brought it with you,' he stated, just as though he knew it for a fact, 'was that you thought this was a safe place in which to sell it.'

Safe place! Sell it! A feeling of nausea invaded her that he could think so of her. 'Would you kindly let go my wrist,' she said coldly. 'Contrary to your delightful opinion

of me, I'm particular who paws me about.' His cynical
disbelieving look was the last straw, and burnt off the rein
she was keeping on her temper. 'Let go my wrist,' she
said, raising her voice, then hissing again when she
became aware of the stares as the crockery on the table
bounced when she tried to get free. 'For your information,
Mr Know-it-all Gray, I have no intention of selling that
ring. And for your further information, the only reason I
brought it with me is that my flat was broken into just
before I left England, and I thought it too valuable to
leave lying around.'

He didn't comment on the ring's value even though she
was expecting some acid remark on how she, a working girl
had got it. Instead an alert look came to his eyes. Then
suddenly, the sun was coming out for her again. For without
warning, he smiled, eased his grip on her wrist, his thumb
starting to caress it as though he knew he had hurt her.

'Forgive me, Laurie,' he said out of the blue. And while
her temper began to evaporate at the change in him, he
said, 'I didn't mean to let you get to me, but for all my
efforts to keep everything platonic between us, I'm
afraid—you have.'

Her heart pounding in her breast, Laurie had no intention of leaving now, as, stuck fast to her seat, she stared
and just stared.

'What—what do you mean?' she managed, then heard
the sound of his anger, and for once, was thrilled by it.

'Good God,' he said tautly, 'surely you know? Surely
you have some idea of the torment I've endured? Coming
into that damned bedroom night after night; seeing you
there asleep. Don't you have any idea of the war that has
raged in me not to get into that bottom bunk with you?'

Pink surged in her cheeks, happiness bubbling. She
almost spat out there and then how the ring came to be
in her possession. That was until she realised it was only
his male chemistry that had him wanting to join her in

that bed. She had heard that some men who through their work were forced to spend nights in hotels—or in Tyler's case, have other accommodation arranged for him—had a reputation for the way they assuaged their loneliness, their boredom when away from home. Not that she could ever imagine Tyler being lonely, but relief from boredom she didn't want to be, any more than she wanted to be put down as just a holiday fling. Now more than ever, with him coming out into the open about his desire for her, she had to keep quiet about that ring, she realised. It was the only thing that had him climbing into that top bunk. Once she had told him there would be nothing in his opinion of her to have him thinking better of it. For she knew herself too weak to resist him should he make any attempt to join her in her bunk.

She clutched hold of her bag, knowing she had to get up and leave. Knowing their days together had to end here—and before night fell.

But as he saw her intention, his grip on her wrist tightened again. 'You are meeting someone?' he suggested quietly, making her despair that despite all that had been revealed he thought she had arranged to meet someone for the purpose of selling the ring. That despair had her not wanting to fight with him any more.

'No—No, I'm not,' she denied, and, honesty to the fore, 'But—but in view of what you've admitted, I—I think the less we see of each other the better.'

'That means you want me as much as I want you—am I right?' His honesty was crucifying hers, made her weak, powerless to stand. 'But even while wanting me too, there's something in you that has you resisting while the donor of that ring has prior claim?'

She wished he'd shut up about the ring, it seemed to bother him as much as carrying it around bothered her. 'It wouldn't be right,' she said, and didn't care what interpretation he put on that, though from the look of him he didn't think too much of her answer.

How could it be right, she thought, to cheapen the love she felt for him by making herself available to him for nothing more than a one-night stand as far as he was concerned? How could she let him make love to her tonight knowing that once her plane had taken off tomorrow he would already have written *finis* to the whole episode?

Tyler looked at her steadily for long moments. Then the grimness in him was letting up, and suddenly he was bringing out a compromise.

'If I abide by the rules, keep my emotions to myself the way I've done all this week, then will you spend the day with me?' She wanted to say yes straight away, and was fighting an inner battle to say no, until he added, 'Will you help me make today as enjoyable as the last three days have been?'

Sunk without trace, Laurie tried not to sound too eager. 'If you think we should,' she said carefully.

'I do,' he said at once, taking his hand from her wrist, only to bring it back to rub the red mark he had left behind. 'More than that, I think today should be your choice.' He smiled a friendly smile. 'Where would you like to go?'

Happiness bursting inside, she knew where she wanted to go, knew she would love it, that he would hate it. She had to bite her lip to stop from laughing. 'Could we go a ride on a sampan?' She laughed out loud at his groan, but all he said was:

'Do you want to go home for your camera?'

No point, she'd run out of film. 'No, thanks,' she said.

By taxi they went to the typhoon shelter in Aberdeen, Tyler looking as though he was enjoying himself as they sat side by side in cane chairs aboard a sampan, although Laurie suspected he wasn't. It was an eye-opener to her as they toured past water craft homes, skyscrapers and green hills forming a backcloth. She jumped, and laughed with Tyler when as they passed one of the craft some kind of miniature terrier suddenly appeared and began yapping at them.

'Look there!' she couldn't help exclaiming when her disbelieving eyes saw on the same craft the small wooden box that had been appended to the side, holding baby chicks that couldn't possibly be more than a week old.

From Aberdeen they went to a market in Stanley, and Laurie saw many china ornaments that would have tempted her had she been more affluent. She chose not to let her eyes linger on anything for too long. With Tyler thinking the way he did about her, she'd just die if he saw she wanted something and bought for her.

'Seen anything you fancy?' he thought to ask when having been all round the market they were ready to leave.

'Not a thing,' she lied.

'What about that silk scarf I saw you admiring?'

'It was nice, wasn't it?' she said offhandedly. 'I bought one in China that was very similar.' That she had bought it for Mei Lai he would never know.

'Sure you wouldn't like another?'

'Look, Tyler,' she said seriously, stopping and looking up at him, 'you're doing enough for me now without putting me further in your debt.' She saw him frown that she was again referring to his charity. 'And—to be blunt,' she went on stubbornly, 'I should feel any gift you made me was given because you thought I'd angled for it.'

'Which only goes to prove how little you know me,' he retorted. Which was true, she owned, because he seemed reluctant to talk about himself. The few facts she knew about him had taken days to find out. 'Had you known me better,' he went on, not knowing it was her dearest wish, 'you would know I only give where I want to give.'

'Well, we don't have to fight about it, do we?' she asked, a glow starting to kindle that it looked as though he had *wanted* to give her a present.

Looking as though he hadn't finished fighting yet, Tyler

looked into her earnest green eyes and saw she was afraid their day was going to be ruined.

'No, we don't,' he agreed. 'Let's go and have lunch.'

Happy again, Laurie sat at a table with him in a Chinese restaurant, wiping her hands on the hot towels that had been brought to the table. She smiled at him as she took her chopsticks out of the sealed envelope they arrived in, then began tucking in to the hors d'oeuvres of sweet cucumber and nuts.

'Steady on,' Tyler cautioned when after having placed several prawns and some sort of egg concoction on to the thinnest of pancakes she helped herself to slivers of onion, all to be parcelled up and eaten. 'That onion is fairly hot.'

She took his advice, and limited her first pancake parcel to only two slivers of onion. It was delicious—more onion and it would have burnt her mouth. Jasmine tea was served throughout the meal, but she knew she was in for something different when a tall silver pot was brought to the table.

'Wine?' Tyler asked, and at her nod, he poured her a glass.

'It's hot,' she said, her fingers taking the warm glass.

'*Gong bouy*,' he toasted her, the equivalent of 'Cheers', she suspected, and knew from the schoolboy grin on his face that she wasn't going to like it.

'You don't have to finish it,' he said, when after a few sips she put down her glass. 'I just thought the experience would appeal to you.'

It just showed, she mused as she sampled the long pastry-looking object placed before her, finding it was filled with minced pork, taking him at his word and leaving the wine, that Tyler had learnt far more about her than she had learned about him.

So full she couldn't eat another morsel, she was in complete agreement when he suggested they walk their meal off.

Today, for all its shaky start, was turning out to be just as good as those other days she had spent in his company, she thought, as without hurrying they walked, talked about nothing in particular, and walked some more.

They were near the sea, at Repulse Bay, when he suggested they take a walk on the sands. The sun was hot, a beautiful day in more ways than one. And so sublimely happy was she just to be with him, she would have fallen in with anything he said.

There were not many people about, and Tyler led the way to a deserted patch of sand. 'I think we've earned a rest,' he said. And when he sat down, so did she, full of him, though she tried to let it seem it was the sandy crescent, the green hills, that held all her attention. Then she felt his eyes on her, felt tense where she hadn't been tense before, and just had to say something, anything.

'Maurice, my boss, said something about this bay being named after a British man-o'-war,' came from her hurriedly. Then, remembering too late that the day had nearly come to grief when she had spoken of her boss before, she darted a quick look at him.

He was giving her a hard-eyed stare, frowning as though he objected to anything to do with her boss. Laurie frowned too. Tyler wasn't jealous of Maurice, she knew that; she would have been thrilled had he been. But clearly he didn't want to be reminded of him either. Not wanting to take issue with him and so spoil the day, she searched around for some other subject, realising that while they were walking, talk had come easily. But sitting down with him like this, she felt suddenly constrained.

'Mei Lai must have been meaning to borrow a camp bed,' she drew out of thin air, and wanted to groan that that was the best she could come up with. But having got started she had to continue when Tyler made the effort to look as though he was if not ecstatic by her comment, then at least doing his best to sound interested.

'Oh? he queried.

'There were to be three of us if things had gone as arranged,' she ploughed on. 'So she would have been one bed short.'

His expression changed, hardened. 'It would have been a mite overcrowded if your friend hadn't decided to stay with her grandmother,' he agreed, adding coldly, 'Perhaps it's just as well your other friend couldn't make it either.'

What was the matter with him? Two minutes ago they had been sitting here quite pleasantly, she had thought. Trying not to get cross, Laurie went back over what she had said, trying to see what, if anything, she had said to make him so broody. He hadn't liked her bringing Maurice's name up, but he had got over that, or had seemed to. Then like a clap of thunder she recalled that day she had sat with him in that café at the Great Wall. She had told him then that her friend couldn't make it, and he—he had made some sour remark about her friend being a married man!

'The—the friend I was going to come on holiday with was a—a girl,' she said, her heart pounding, that ridiculous idea coming to her—was he jealous? Or had she again made a fool of herself by stressing the sex of her friend?

His look didn't lighten, so that she knew she had. 'Let you down at the last minute, did she?' he remarked, his look disbelieving.

'It wasn't her fault,' she answered, growing cool herself, that or start to be angry. 'Kay was taken into hospital the day before we were due to come away. I told you my flat was broken into—it happened while I was out visiting her.'

Would she never keep up with him? Laurie wondered. For as suddenly as he had turned into a man who had her fighting to keep calm, he was back again to being a charming companion. 'I'm a grouch sometimes, aren't I?' he asked, that charm skittling her.

'It probably stems from something that happened in

your childhood,' she trotted out, knowing the way he so quickly changed mood was infectious, for suddenly she no longer felt cold towards him. She was happy again now his black patch had disappeared.

'Going to forgive me?'

'If you don't let it happen again,' she said, laughing inside.

'I'll be a model of good behaviour from now on,' he promised, the sun for her in his smile. 'I'll take you for a cup of tea in a minute, and since it's your day let you decide where you'd like to go for dinner tonight.'

'I don't know anywhere,' she answered, since the only times she had dined out had been places he had chosen. 'Wait a minute, though. . . .' Suddenly she was diving into her bag searching for her wallet. 'I've just remembered, Maurice——' damn, his name had slipped out again! She kept her face towards her bag, not wanting to see if his expression had changed. 'He—er—wrote down the name of a restaurant he insisted I should try.'

She had her hands on her wallet now, but wasn't at all sure Tyler would want to take her anywhere near the place her boss had suggested.

'Are you going to tell me where it is?' Tyler asked, keeping to his word that he was going to be a model of good behaviour.

Oh hell, what was she afraid of? Laurie wondered as she resisted the impulse to say she had lost the piece of paper. She wanted Tyler to stay nice to her, but if she went on like this, wasn't she in danger of losing her own identity?

She extracted the many times folded quarto sheet she had forgotten to transfer to her Hong Kong wallet as she had intended, and opened it out to see Maurice's familiar scrawl covering it.

'It's somewhere in the Wanchai district,'she said, 'but I've no idea where.'

'Let's have a look,' said Tyler, taking the paper from her. 'I know it,' he said, casting his eyes over the address and handing the paper back to her. 'It's a very. . . .' He broke off, frown lines appearing as his brows drew together.

The paper had been in her hand when, without apology, rudely, he snatched it from her and turned it over.

'What this?' he asked sharply, scanning what looked to her like so many hieroglyphics on the back.

'What's what?' she asked in return, peering over his shoulder. 'Oh, that. It looks like the Professor's writing. It can't be important—only jottings—otherwise it would have been put in the safe.'

Tyler too had seen it was nothing more than the Professor's scribble, she thought. He had gone off the idea of tea as well, she mused, for folding the paper over, without more ado he lay back on the sands and closed his eyes.

She wished he hadn't mentioned tea. For where before she hadn't felt thirsty, Laurie was starting to think she could drink a gallon. Though since Tyler would be paying, she didn't like to remind him of his offer.

'All the important papers are kept in the safe, are they?' he asked, when she had thought he would soon be asleep, that he had forgotten all about her work. What reason he had for snatching that piece of scrap out of her hand she didn't know, but it was enough that his voice was remaining easy as he spoke about her place of employment.

'Oh yes,' she said, deciding it was better not to mention Maurice's name after all. 'Alastair is most particular about that—Alastair's the Professor, though of course we're all very security-conscious.'

'Does Alastair, this Professor, often come into your office?' he asked, his eyes closed still.

Laurie allowed herself a few moments to wonder, since

she had discounted that he was jealous of Maurice, if it could possibly be that he didn't like the idea of Alastair coming in to see her frequently.

'He's in every day,' she said, knowing if Tyler could see him, spectacles perched on top of his head, his lined face looking older than his years, he would know he had no cause to be jealous.

Her heart was drumming away, she just had to find out if she was on the right tack. And she babbled on for some minutes about their tame professor, since Tyler hadn't once opened his eyes having freedom to search for any change in his expression.

But with his eyes hidden, there was no change, even though she went on about the Professor being about the same age as he was, being a love, and how well she got on with him.

'He came into the office on my last day,' she ended, wanting him to think he had come in specially to see her.

'To wish you a happy holiday?' He called her bluff. And she just couldn't lie.

'Er—well, no, actually.' Then, recalling the excitement of that afternoon, she told him how Alastair, after months of painstaking work, had stumbled across a certain momentous breakthrough just that day, and of the congratulations afterwards.

She then discovered that Tyler wasn't jealous at all. He had merely been showing a polite interest, and that if the occasional grunt that came her way was anything to go by, she was boring him to tears with her talk of work.

Feeling not only disappointed, but also that she had made a fool of herself again, she felt her spirits lighten when after she told him the Professor's findings had been safely locked up in the safe, Tyler roused himself to tease:

'Did he put these very important papers in the safe before or after—er—Maurice gave you the address of his favourite restaurant?'

Laurie looked away, sure his lips would be twitching. She had rather gone on a bit, hadn't she, seeing that since he hadn't felt the atmosphere of Craye & Co, he couldn't be expected to appreciate the major step forward the discovery had been.

'He didn't put them in the safe, I did,' she said, her own lips starting to twitch. She could play this teasing game as long as him. 'Alastair is about as tidy as Maurice, and his desk always looks like an unmade bed. Alastair went to phone the big chief, I found a file and put his papers away, then Maurice found a sheet of scrap to write that address down.'

She looked at Tyler then, and saw he was smiling broadly, and loved him the more that he felt friends enough with her to tease her so outrageously.

Though she wasn't so very sure of his teasing when his grin faded and he asked, 'These findings of the Professor's—what were they about?'

She knew it was to do with a preventative formula to do with metal erosion, but that was about as much as she did know. But she found then that as much as she loved Tyler, she couldn't even tell him that much. He was ribbing her, sending her up as he had done before. And she knew it was solely because she had given him the impression that she thought the work her firm did was far more important than the work anyone else's firm did. But even so. . . .

'I—I'm sorry, Tyler,' she said quietly, 'I can't tell you. I—I'm not employed by Craye & Company because I'm a—a blabbermouth.'

The reaction her prim remark aroused in him startled her so much it had her heart pounding in her ears. Abruptly he sat up, his face split from ear to ear.

'Laurie Frost, I love you,' he said. And while her heart thundered, he stood up, his hand stretched down to her.

CHAPTER NINE

THEY didn't dine at the restaurant Maurice had recommended, although Tyler had pocketed the address, probably to refresh his memory, Laurie had thought. Nor did he follow up his statement that he loved her.

As she thought her heart would burst he had pulled her to her feet and folded her in his arms. Incapable of speech, she had just stood and stared at him, then felt him push her away. 'It's hell to remember you're only out with me today because of my promise to keep it platonic,' he had said ruefully, when she wanted to tell him to forget all about the promise. Then casually, so she knew he hadn't meant it when he had said he loved her, 'Let's go and find that cup of tea.'

His mood had been light after that, carefree almost. And though he must never know of her deep disappointment, Laurie joined in with his mood, seeing his comment for what it had been. She had tickled his sense of humour with what he saw as her quaint loyalty to the firm she worked for. Her prim refusal to tell him what the professor's discovery had been about, just as though she suspected him of being a foreign agent at least—well, her firm did work on a few government projects—must have had him highly amused. It tickled her, now she came to think of it.

They dined at the Peak, Hong Kong and Kowloon lit up with a million lights, craft ferrying to and fro way down there below them. And even if Tyler didn't love her, Laurie was happy. For their meal together that night was different. She couldn't quite put her finger on why. It could have been that it all stemmed from Tyler's light mood. She had enjoyed meals with him before, but tonight there seemed to be added some intangible new dimension. She stopped ferreting at it, and gave herself up to enjoying her last night with him, enjoying the way he was making it appear he was more than happy to have her for a dinner partner.

'Shall we take a taxi home?' he consulted her after they left the restaurant.

Knowing that if they went home now she would have to go straight to bed, the evening at an end, Laurie tried to think up a way to spend more time in his company.

'Or would you rather walk some of your dinner off first?' he unknowingly helped her out.

'Perhaps it would be a good idea,' she said, and felt the sorest disappointment when he hailed a taxi just the same.

That was until the taxi stopped and she didn't recognise at all where they were.

'Thought you might like to take a look round an open-air night market,' said Tyler, helping her to alight. 'We're not far from home, we can walk the rest of the way.'

In a dream world, having his hand holding on to her arm so they shouldn't get separated in the crush, Laurie strolled round the market with him. Sights, sounds, various smells all registering while she was above all over-whelmingly aware of Tyler.

They stopped at a stall where a refreshment vendor was stewing away some white dumpling sort of things in unmentionable grey-looking water.

'Want to try some?' Tyler asked, and Laurie just knew there was a dare in his question.

'We could try a bowl between us,' she answered, throwing down a gauntlet of her own.

Her laugh just missed being a giggle when without batting an eye Tyler negotiated with the cook. Then he was handing her one of the two china spoons he had in his hand and inviting her to partake from the bowl where about eight of the small dumplings lodged.

'Ladies first,' he said with a grin, and there was nothing for it but to take one.

'Delicious,' she said, having meant to say that even if they were foul. Then as the sweet taste of caramel livened her taste buds, 'They really are!' and loved him the more when lightly his finger came to tap her nose.

Leaving the market, they turned into darker streets, and Laurie was startled when they came across a settee tucked into one of the side streets, its down-and-out occupant sound asleep.

'Fresh air fiend,' said Tyler, and it seemed the most natural thing in the world then for him to place an arm about her shoulders. He kept his arm about her until they reached Mei Lai's building.

'Thank you for a wonderful day,' Laurie said softly, when they went into the apartment.

'I enjoyed it too,' he said quietly, his eyes searching hers.

'I'll—I'll use the bathroom first,' she choked, tension heavy in her. Then she knew Tyler was remembering his promise to keep everything platonic, when he looked away to where he had placed his paperback.

'Might finish the last chapter tonight if I'm lucky,' he murmured, and left her to go and get her things from the bedroom.

She showered and cleaned her teeth, her happiness of the evening dimming fast. There had been a sort of finality in Tyler when he had said he would finish the last chapter tonight. It was as though he was saying that after tonight it would all be ended.

Laurie belted her robe, picked up her sponge bag, then trying to keep her face from showing how down she was suddenly feeling, she stepped from the bathroom.

'Goodnight,' she said lightly, the bedroom only two steps away.

'Goodnight, Laurie,' Tyler replied evenly, already deep in his reading, but looking up briefly to see her shining newly scrubbed face.

Her feet wanted to go forward towards him, but she quickly turned them, and in a second was quietly closing the bedroom door.

Tomorrow she had to say goodbye to him. Oh, how was she going to do that without breaking down? But she mustn't do that. Whatever happened she mustn't let him see how her heart was aching inside.

She snagged her nail when going to put her toilet bag out of the way down by their cases, and sat on the edge of her bunk while she found a nail file in her bag, then smoothed off the roughened part. And it was as she was returning the file to her bag that she saw again the ring box Maurice had left in her safe keeping.

She took it out, opened the box and stared pensively at the ring, remembering because of that sparkling object Tyler's opinion of her was lower than low. He had successfully hidden what he thought of her morals today, she thought, and couldn't help her mind drifting back to that time at Repulse Bay that afternoon. She recalled without effort the way he had said, 'Laurie Frost, I love you,' and suddenly her pulses were leaping. Even having rationalised that it had meant precisely nothing, she was choking as she wondered, was Tyler the sort of man who went around telling a girl he loved her when he didn't mean it?

Her heart began to hammer whether she was fooling herself or not. He had told her very little about himself, but she hadn't lived under the same roof with him, gone everywhere with him this last few days without learning that he rarely said anything he didn't mean. He just *wasn't* the sort of man who carelessly, willy-nilly, dropped out those three little words that meant so much.

The beat of her heart was threatening to choke her, had her gasping for a short breath as realisation came that he would never say more than that while that ring was between them. That if he did love her—oh, God, please not let her be fooling herself—then she had done nothing, said nothing, to let him know she had never taken anything from a man in return for favours given.

She had to tell him, tell him the truth about that ring, she thought, trying to swallow down the excitement that rioted in her. She had to tell him, and since it wouldn't wait until the morning, she had to tell him—now.

Laurie closed the lid on the ring and dropped it back into her bag, fastening it with a snap as she tried to go against the urge that was in her to go into the other room and explain. She would be calmer in the morning, she reasoned, more able to take it if after she had told Tyler everything he merely said, 'Sorry I jumped to the wrong conclusion,' and left it at that.

She made herself sit down on her bunk again. But it was only for a few seconds. He *had* said I love you. She just couldn't wait until tomorrow to find out if it had been the throwaway remark she had thought it to be.

Quietly, her heart going like galloping hooves, Laurie opened the bedroom door. Tyler was sat on the settee with his book open before him, but he wasn't reading. He was deep in thought, she thought. She took a step forward and his head jerked round—no hostility there, she saw, searching to find a smile for him when committed now, but her throat had dried up. That was until Tyler found his voice first and helped her out.

'I—was just thinking about you,' he said softly, his eyes flicking from her face over her robe and back again.

'N-nice th-thoughts, I hope,' she said, her nervousness showing.

For answer he stretched his hand over the back of the settee to her. Laurie went forward, her heart jumping, electricity shooting up her arm as she placed her hand in his.

'Come and sit here beside me,' he said, holding on to her hand and bringing her round to sit beside him on the small settee.

Unable to look at his lest he see from her eyes the way things were with her, Laurie sat looking down at her knees, wondering where she should start.

'Er—you—you said you were thinking about me,' she said huskily, the words she wanted to tell him about the ring not presenting themselves.

'About you,' Tyler said close to her ear, 'and—about us.'

'Us?'

Joy, hope broke, her head spun round. She found his face was just a fraction away, looked dumbly into his dark brown eyes, and saw the light in them turn to fire that she was this close.

'Oh, hell,' he groaned, his arm coming about her. 'You've got to let me break my promise, Laurie. I shall go mad if I don't kiss you soon!'

She moved that fraction closer, the way her arms went up and around him as his lips met hers all the evidence he needed that she wanted him to break that promise to keep things platonic as much as he did.

It was heaven to be in his arms, to have his mouth covering her face in tiny kisses, to have his lips finding hers again, drawing from her her very soul.

'Laurie darling,' he breathed, to her utter enchantment, and his arms pulled her closer, pressing her to him. He groaned as though his lips had been too long away from hers, kissing her again and again, drawing a fire she had never thought she was capable of.

'Oh, Tyler!' she whispered when he broke his kiss, his mouth searching in the hollows of her throat, his hands sending her into mindless ecstasy as he caressed and had her yearning for him.

Again he kissed her, bringing a moan from her when at last his hands found her breasts, his fingers circling the hardened tip.

'Do you need to wear this thing?' he muttered, his voice thick in his throat as he undid the tie of her robe, discarding it, pushing her nightdress down over her shoulders.

The feel of his lips on her naked skin had her heady with desire, had her unbuttoning his shirt, her hands tormenting in the roughened hair of his chest.

His mouth captured hers again, his hands on her hips pressing her to him. Then his mouth was at her breast, one arm somehow out of her nightdress allowing him to pull the material down. Colour surged in her face when she saw his look go from her to the firm crimson-tipped mound of her breast.

'You're beautiful. Oh, God, you're so beautiful,' he said, his voice husky. And as if unable to look and not savour, his mouth was at her breast, his tongue sending frantic flames of desire shooting through her as it roved the peak made more prominent by his sensitive touch. His hand captured her naked swelling breast as he kissed her again, his other arm tight about her as he tried to press her harder to his need for her, moving her on the short settee, his frustration showing as he tried to lie with her and was hampered.

'This must be the most uncomfortable settee on record,' he said softly.

Laurie's passion was finding new heights and it was only shyness with him that had her holding back the suggestion that they would be more comfortable in the other room. And then Tyler was looking deep into her eyes, his face flushed as she knew hers to be.

'I want you, darling,' he breathed. 'Will you be mine?'

'Oh, Tyler,' she choked, knowing he must see the answer there in her eyes, in her love-flushed face. 'Yes,

—yes,' she agreed willingly.

He kissed her once more, then stood holding her in his arms, looking down at her as though she was something more than special. Then bending his head, he kissed her creamy breast, carrying her into the bedroom to where not only had she left the light on, but as he bent to lower her on her bunk, she saw her solid handbag in the way.

'We won't be needing that,' he said softly, and with his eyes fixed to hers he picked up her bag and aimed it to land on top of their cases against the wall.

The terrific clatter that followed, as the balance of the suitcases was disturbed and the cases came skidding along the floor, brought a smile to Laurie's mouth. Her case caught Tyler's leg, but he ignored it, his eyes on her as he shrugged off any pain encountered.

Her smile changed to one of shyness as she saw his hot gaze move to where somehow in their move from the settee both her breasts were now exposed to his look. Her face glowing, she looked away from the naked passion she saw in him, for a moment too delirious with her own heady need to take in what her eyes were seeing in the shape of Tyler's suitcase; open from its fall, the contents spread about.

The mattress safely under her, Tyler kissed her, left her only briefly while he went to switch out the light.

Laurie's voice, the puzzlement in it, the strangeness, reached him as he returned to gather her to him, his intention not being fulfilled as he complied with her hesitating request:

'Would—would you put the light on again?'

Light flooded the room, a question in his eyes that said he hadn't missed the curious oddness of her tone. But Laurie didn't see that question. Her eyes were elsewhere. Open-mouthed, she stared at her wallet—the wallet she had last seen in China but which had now slipped out from the folds of one of his shirts.

Trying desperately hard with what brain power he had left her with, Laurie looked from the wallet to Tyler as she sought for comprehension. His jaw was clenched she saw as he too hadn't missed seeing what had caused her to ask him to put the light on again.

'Th-that's my wallet!' she gasped. 'The one—that was stolen!' came whispering from her.

'It is,' he confirmed. 'Darling. . . .'

'But—but what's it doing in your case?' she asked, her overheated blood cooling as she fought through the mists of her confusion. Then, aghast, 'You—you didn't—steal it!' Wondering if she was going crazy, Laurie stared transfixed at her wallet. Nothing was making sense.

Even with the evidence there in front of her, her wallet appearing from nowhere other than Tyler's case, she couldn't believe it. Her emotions, her need, were so aroused by him, she wasn't sure even with that evidence that she wouldn't have believed him had he denied taking it.

But Tyler did not deny it. 'Laurie. My dear,' he said, 'I can explain. . . .'

'Explain?' Oh no! Oh, dear God, no! 'It was *you*!' she whispered hoarsely, shock hitting her, hitting her hard as it came to bring her out of her lost to the world state. 'It was you,' she croaked, cowering as he tried to come near her, her need for him dead, only sad, sad disappointment in its place.

And it was then, as Tyler pulled back as though he thought her cowering meant she feared him, never so shattered in her life, that a different passion began to take possession of her. She was on her feet, righting her night-dress on her shoulders, her eyes starting to smoulder, as, her voice rising, she cried:

'You! You stole it!'

Whether he thought she was on the way to becoming hysterical Laurie neither knew nor cared, but in contrast to hers, his voice was calm as he said quietly:

'There is an explanation. . . .'

'I'll bet there is,' she said bitterly, and with the thought, My God, another few minutes and she would have . . . and she was yelling, 'You liar! You cheat!' seeing his eyes glint that he didn't like her becalling him, but she was so enraged it mattered nothing to her that he didn't like the truth. She had found him out for a thief and it made a nonsense of her reasoning that he had meant anything at all when he had said he loved her. That thought brought pain, quieted her threatening hysteria, quieted her voice that had been on the point of shrieking. 'How could you?' she asked huskily, the bleeding hurt wounding.

'If you will listen I'll. . . .'

'I'm not interested in your lies!' she cut him off—she had to, knew herself all too vulnerable to anything he said.

'I don't intend to lie,' he said shortly, just as though, she thought, it was she in the wrong, not him! Wasn't that what his sort did, gave you a story so plausible you ended up apologising for ever having doubted them?

She looked down at his spilled out case, saw the indisputable evidence there before her eyes. 'My God,' she breathed, not wanting to believe it, 'you're nothing but a con-man!'

Searing disillusionment had her in its grip as she saw just how gullible she had been, saw how green Tyler must have thought her. He must have been laughing up his sleeve that not once had she thought to question him. Even when she had found her wallet missing—in this very flat, Tyler there for her to question—not once had she thought to refer to that time she had seen him coming out of her room in China.

'You stole it in Peking,' she accused flatly. 'That morning you said you were doing your bit for East-West relations.' She didn't need him to confirm it, she saw bitterly how easily she had been duped, saw just how practised he must be. 'You must be the biggest smoothie of all time!' she reviled him, uncaring that her bitterness was showing. 'The floor boy wouldn't so much as let me tip him for my laundry, yet you managed to bribe him to let you into my room.'

'I didn't bribe him,' he told her, his voice sounding tough. 'I told him you were my fiancée, that we'd had a row and that I wanted to leave a present for you.' Smooth wasn't the word, Laurie thought as he went on, an angry edge coming to her, surmounting that flat feeling that had hold of her. 'He'd already done your room, he wasn't likely to go looking to see what I'd left.'

Pain was rocking her that he was so unconcerned he could even tell her how he had been able to do it. 'But you didn't leave anything, did you? You took instead.'

'I've said I can explain.'

'Explain!' Laurie jumped in, no explanation in her book excusing that he was nothing more than a common crook. 'You can keep your explanations, I'm not interested,' she flared, too aware that she was more vulnerable than that floor boy to his quick-talking tongue. And, glad to feel her temper biting again, she wouldn't let him get a word in as hot words flew. 'I'll bet you thought you'd hit the jackpot when I walked through the door of this flat!'

'Jackpot?'

She didn't believe the expression on his face that said he had no idea what she was talking about. 'You fancied having a *fling* with me in China, didn't you? You knew damn well when I walked through that door that I was broke—knew if you played your cards right there might be a big seduction scene at the end of it.'

'Seduction scene?' he echoed, then added insult to injury. 'Don't talk rot!'

'*Rot!*'

Her temper getting out of hand as her dormant intelligence roared into life, Laurie saw that everything he said and did had to be questioned. Things she had seen no need to question before, all were now suspect.

'And it's rot too, is it, that you couldn't change my plane ticket?'

'I didn't try. I didn't go near the airport that day. I didn't think you seriously intended that I should,' he had the utter gall to tell her.

'So it was the big seduction scene you were after,' she accused. And as his, 'I didn't think you seriously intended that I should,' sorted itself out in her brain, 'Why, you conceited . . .! You had the nerve to think I was already half way ready to get into bed with you—that by the time it came for me to go home I'd be panting to go all the way with you!'

She saw he was getting angry too, but she didn't care. If he so much as hinted that it had looked that way to him, she wasn't sure she wouldn't be hurling herself at him ready to scratch his eyes out.

'I didn't plan the bedroom scene,' he told her, keeping his anger in check. 'It—just happened that way.'

But she was too furious to care what he said any more. She wouldn't now believe him whatever he said. She felt nauseated by it all, devastated that her trust in him had been abused.

Wanting to be alone to lick her wounds, she bent to his case, tossing the spilled contents in anyhow, then sent it skidding speedily across the floor and into the other room.

'If you possess so much as an atom of decency in your dark soul,' she flung at him, picking up a shirt and an odd shoe and throwing them out after his case, 'then you'll do me the courtesy of allowing me to be the sole occupant of this room.'

Tyler didn't like the way she was maltreating his belongings, she could see, either that or he objected to being forced to spend the night sleeping on that crippling settee. For the check on his anger broke.

'Decency!' he snarled, surprising her, with his record, that the word had obviously stung. 'Who the hell are you to talk of decency?' He was at the door, having shocked her into silence since she didn't understand his meaning, and had only one thing to say before he strode to the other side of the door, closing it and leaving her with the cold comfort of solitude. 'At least *I* don't go around trying to break up marriages!'

By what right did he assume she was trying to break up a marriage? Laurie thought, trying to sustain her anger. But it was no good, she felt more like breaking her heart now he wasn't around for her to fire up at. In his book, obviously, especially since she had told him she wasn't engaged, he had assumed the donor of that ring must be married, otherwise she would be able to wear it openly.

What did she care what he thought anyway? she wondered, as she lay wide awake on her bunk. Talk about nursing a viper to her bosom—a viper wasn't in it! She had been right to think she had made a fool of herself over him, she must be the biggest fool of all time. To think she had been so in love with him she hadn't even considered the possibility that it could be he who had stolen her money, when that possibility had been staring her in the face all along.

Well, all she hoped was that he was finding that settee twice—no, three times as uncomfortable as she had found it, she thought, and tears started to her eyes.

It proved a long night for Laurie, the longest night she had ever spent. Long-drawn-out minutes ticked slowly by with her brain too over-active to find sleep. Thank God she had found out about him before . . . before rather than after, her thoughts sped on, unable to deny that that cheap crook's lovemaking had fired that something new in her.

It was nearly dawn when her spinning head found relief from the torment of her thoughts in sleep. But she was not at all surprised when she woke a few hours later with a splitting head.

Lying there wouldn't make it any better, she thought, sitting up. And then found temporary relief from her headache in the surprise that met her eyes in the shape of her dressing gown she had last seen when Tyler had so expertly taken it from her shoulders.

Hot colour surged through her face at the memory of how she had been putty in his hands. Well, she wouldn't be putty in his hands this morning, she determined, shrugging into her robe, adding cat burglar to his list of crimes, for she hadn't heard him bring it in.

She tightened her belt, took from her case the things she was going to travel home in, then opened the bedroom door ready for him if he said just one single solitary word to her.

But when she stepped into the living room, she found her intention to treat him just as though he didn't exist wasn't needed. For Tyler was not there.

She looked round for the case she had so furiously ejected from the bedroom, but that wasn't there either. The bathroom door stood open and there was no one in the kitchen.

And there on the table she saw her wallet. She went over and picked it up, checked the contents. It was all there, every dollar, every traveller's cheque.

So he had found a grain of decency in his black heart, she thought, her intention to wash and get dressed diminishing. She sat at the table, tears she had no use for spilling down her face. So he had gone. And she was glad. Oh, hell, why then was she crying!

CHAPTER TEN

OTHER people had been able to sleep on that fifteen-hour flight home, Laurie thought as she entered her flat, so why hadn't she? She had been tired enough, goodness knew. She felt now that if she slept for a week it still wouldn't be long enough.

She went to where she kept her asprin and took a couple. She'd had a perpetual headache since she had woken up yesterday morning, but wished she could anaesthetise the ache in her heart so easily.

She still loved him, of course. That fact had come home to her as Tyler, Tyler, Tyler, had spun round in her brain. He must have been staggered, she had reasoned, when he had seen her walk in through Mei Lai's door. He had lifted her wallet and thought he had seen the last of her. Not that his face had shown any reaction that she could remember. But then con men were prepared for any such eventuality, no doubt. And as for him saying he was staying at Mei Lai's flat because he hated hotel life, it was probably nearer the truth, since pilfering in hotels was his side line, that the hotels in Hong Kong were most likely getting wise to him and that he dared not show his face in any of them.

Listlessly, her headache clearing, Laurie got on with her unpacking, coming across the presents she had brought back. She would have to phone her parents soon to let them know she'd arrived safely, and Kay too, she thought. But where she was going to dredge up some sort of happy enthusiasm she had no idea.

Again her thoughts went back to Tyler, finding no relief or satisfaction that since money must be his god, he had been the one to end up out of pocket. For not only had he fed her and taken her around, he had purposely left her wallet and its contents behind. Perhaps that meant he liked her a little, she thought. That was before anger came, making her furious with herself that she could be such a weakling as to want his liking.

She rang her parents' home, and because she had to sound cheerful, began to feel better.

'You're still coming home next weekend, aren't you?' her mother asked.

'Looking forward to it,' said Laurie. 'Will Jamie be home?'

'He's going to try, but don't dare let him hear you call him Jamie—he thinks now he's at university he's grown out of it!'

The smile that being part of a loving family aroused faded a minute after Laurie had put down the phone. Her mother made everything sound so fundamentally normal—yet love had made her feel she could never be part of that normality again. That never again would she breeze into her old home and tell her father he worked too hard, to shed his slippers and she would take him out for a drink.

Slippers, she thought, and was back in Hong Kong with Tyler remarking that her pretty toes might feel the nip of a cockroach.

Despairing of two minutes passing together without some memory of him popping into her head, she picked up the phone and dialled Kay's number, finding Kay was home and well able to come to the phone. And also that Cupid's dart had been busy elsewhere as Kay barely waited for her to finish saying the trip had been all she hoped before she was telling her about this divine doctor she had met, and had fallen for.

'I'll come over, shall I?' Kay suggested. 'I've simply loads to tell you.'

'Er—I was thinking of going to bed,' Laurie put her off, thinking she just wasn't up to hearing Kay, who because of their great friendship would give her a blow-by-blow account of what being in love was like.

'I expect you're jet-lagged to the eyeballs,' said Kay, not offended. 'It'll have to be Monday, then. Drew has wangled tomorrow off with a promise of Sunday, so I want to keep myself free just in case.'

Laurie was pleased for Kay, and came away from the phone sincerely hoping her friend would never know the heartache of loving unwisely.

Feeling dead on her feet, Laurie went to bed, finding to her surprise when she awoke that she had slept a full eight hours.

Saturday passed slowly. A visit to get in food supplies, when she wasn't hungry, took far less time than she'd hoped. Rinsing through the laundry she had brought back, sprucing up her flat, still left her with too much time to think.

But it was on Sunday, late in the afternoon as she was getting her things ready for work the next day, that Laurie received the greatest shock, that made any other shock she had so far received pale into insignificance.

The suit she intended to wear was pressed and on its hanger, likewise the shirt. Her shoes polished, she went to sort out her handbag. She had been so tied up with her thoughts of Tyler's treachery, Anona's ring hadn't so much as whispered through her mind. But she saw the ring box again as she emptied everything from her bag. She had no idea why she went to open it, for that ring had done her no favours—though maybe it had! Had it not been for that ring Tyler would never have put her down as a 'nothing for nothing' girl, and would have followed up his 'holiday romance' inclines much sooner than he had. He had called her darling, she recalled. . . .

Quite suddenly, in the middle of thinking, oh, damn

Tyler, a feeling of alarm began to prickle along her spine. Oh no! Laurie knew fear. She was suddenly afraid then to lift the lid of the ring box. Suspicion for the first time entered her being. He wouldn't—he couldn't—couldn't have, could he?

Knowing she had to pull back that lid, she remembered finding her dressing gown on the bottom of the bed on Thursday morning—Tyler had visited the room while she slept!

And it was with that remembrance that she was seized by a terrible shaking which made it impossible for several seconds for her to open the box. Her hands moist, her throat dry, she tried for calm, swallowed on fear, and at last was able to prise back the lid. Only to find her worst suspicions were confirmed—the box was empty!!

Ashen-faced, she stared, not wanting to believe it. Then she was hurriedly tipping everything out of her bag, searching on the floor while knowing all the time she wasn't going to find it; for the hinge on that box was firm, and there was not the smallest chance for that ring to have left its velvet bed without the aid of a human hand.

Half an hour later, her face without colour still, Laurie had realised that even after it had been revealed that Tyler wasn't above nipping into her hotel room and stealing from her, there was that in her that still insisted in trusting him.

Had that not been the case she would have slept with the ring under her pillow, or on her hand, but she hadn't. She must still have been trusting him when the very first thing she should have done on finding him gone was to check to see he had not taken the ring with him.

Yet the pain of this latest development had to be got over, Laurie knew. She had to stop thinking of his treachery and decide what she was going to do.

Everything in her upbringing, her own honesty, screamed at her to contact the police and let them sort it out. But her hand just would not go near to the telephone to ring them. Even while telling herself he deserved everything he got, she just could not report him.

A further half hour passed, and it was at the end of that time that Laurie knew just what she was going to do. She was going to find the address of Tyler's firm in Milton Keynes. He might still be in Hong Kong, of course, but she was going to see Bridge Electrics first thing in the morning, and make them, whatever story she had to invent, tell her Tyler's home address.

Her insides churned up as she realised Maurice might start to get anxious about the ring if she wasn't at work in the morning. He wanted that ring to take home on Monday night, didn't he? She couldn't remember then, as sweat stuck her clothes to her, exactly when he had said Anona's birthday was. She would have to telephone him, keep him calm anyway until she had something to tell him. He'd have a blue fit if he thought Anona's birthday surprise was not only ruined, but non-existent.

Knowing his number off by heart, having many times when he was too involved to dial it himself dialled it for him, she was so overwrought she couldn't remember the dialling sequence and had to first check it.

'Mr and Mrs Lancaster are away for the weekend, they won't be back until very late tonight,' Maurice's housekeeper told her when she knew who was calling. 'Can I take a message, Miss Frost?'

'N-no. No, thank you,' Laurie replied, not at all sure where she was. 'It was nothing important.'

She'd have to ring him from a callbox in Milton Keynes tomorrow, she thought, as next she rang directory enquires and waited for them to answer. She intended getting up early and being in Milton Keynes before nine. She could ring Maurice from there to tell him she would be late in.

Directory enquiries answered and Laurie asked for the full address and phone number of Bridge Electrics. She didn't need their phone number, but the operator wasn't to know that.

'Is it a new subscriber?' the operator came back. 'They're not listed in the directory.'

'They must be!' Laurie exclaimed, and remembering Tyler telling her he had worked for them for years, had the operator hunting in every reference book she could think of before she came back to say:

'I'm sorry. If they exist at all, they certainly are not on the phone.'

What sort of firm was it, Laurie wondered, stunned, who sent their buyers as far as Hong Kong to do business, yet did not possess one single telephone? It was impossible for any company to exist without at least one telephone in this day and age, she thought. And then she had to accept that that said it all—Bridge Electrics was just one more instance of Tyler Gray being a con merchant. Bridge Electrics just did not exist!

Trauma was an understatement for what she went through in the next few hours. The clock showed midnight, but it was pointless going to bed only to have nightmares of Maurice tearing his hair out when she told him what she had to tell him when she went into work tomorrow.

Oh God, she groaned, aspirin not the least bit of good in this situation. She had thought living in London had taken away the green edges accumulated in her growing years in the Midlands. But then never in her four years of living in London had she ever come across a shark such as Tyler Gray.

It was going on for one in the morning when she went over ground she had been over countless times. How, if Bridge Electrics did not exist, did the Ting Yat Electronic Company know their representative so well they had offered him the use of Mei Lai's flat while he was in Hong Kong?

Her heart lifted as she half remembered an advertising campaign for new industry in Milton Keynes. Perhaps Tyler's firm had taken over new premises, had started a sudsidiary company under a different name. A different name, but because he had worked for them for 'more years then I care to remember' he automatically gave the name of the firm he had initially worked for.

Laurie glanced at the clock, hope growing as she saw there was a very easy way to find out the name and address of Tyler's firm: Mei Lai could tell her. Quickly she calculated that with Hong Kong being eight hours in front of Greenwich Mean Time, Mei Lai should have started her first day back at work some ten minutes ago.

Careless of the expense in ringing Hong Kong, she recalled seeing the slip of paper with the Ting Yat company's phone number on it when she had tipped her bag out. Tyler had dictated it to her that day. . . . She pushed thoughts of him away as she found the paper and checked to find she could dial Hong Kong direct. Then her fingers got busy, her stubbornness to the fore as she tussled with the Chinese girl at the other end until she eventually got through to her that she wanted to speak with Mei Lai Wong.

'Laurie!' Mei Lai exclaimed excitedly on hearing her. 'I have already written you to thank you so much for the silk scarf you left for me.' And before Laurie could get a word in, she was apologising profusely that she had missed seeing her. 'I'm so sorry,' she went on, 'but I was—how do you say—pulled a couple of ways. Out of the sky the day I am leaving for China my boss is telling me, insisting so I cannot believe it, that I am to have an extra two weeks' holiday—making me feel guilty that I am always thinking he is of skinflint.'

Mei Lai's English was quite good, but they seemed to have their wires crossed somewhere, Laurie thought, re-calling her assumption when Tyler had relayed the news that her grandmother's condition had deteriorated she had thought Mei Lai must have phoned through from China to ask for extra leave.

'You didn't ask for an extension to your holiday when you discovered how ill your grandmother was?'

'No, no,' said Mei Lai. 'I did not know before I went away the way of her illness,' and chirruping on, back to her boss again, 'But with Mr Leung—having guilt feelings about his own grandmother who died recently, I think—making it a condition of the two extra weeks that I stay with my grandmother the whole of my holiday, it meant I should have to miss seeing you and Kay.'

This whole business was getting smellier and smellier, Laurie thought, trying to keep on top of this fresh bewilderment. 'But you *did* arrange with Mr—er—Leung to let one of the buyers from England use your flat while you were away?'

'This is a bad line,' said Mei Lai, clearly not understanding her. 'I thought you said I had arranged through Mr Leung to let my flat to someone else.' She laughed gaily at what she thought was a mistake, 'The flat in relation to your flats in England is small, as you must see. It is only big enough for my mother and me. That is what decided me that I must miss seeing you this time—because I wanted you and Kay not to feel crowded. The concierge told you this, though, did he not? I was not sure in my mind before I went away, but after thinking about it I telephoned him especially to tell him this was the reason I would be staying with my grandmother for two more weeks, and for him to explain this to my two English visitors.'

What Mei Lai was saying about the message the concierge should have given her and Kay went over Laurie's head as she pressed the point more important to her.

'You did *not* arrange for anyone else to stay in the flat while. . . .' she began to press, speaking slowly just in case

Mei Lai had misinterpreted her the first time.

'Of course not,' Mei Lai burst in, then her laughter faded. 'Something is wrong, Laurie?'

'Nothing to worry about,' said Laurie promptly, hanging grimly on, one last question buzzing around in her brain she wanted the answer to. 'Mei Lai,' she said, trying to keep her voice light, 'would you do me a favour?'

'Anything at all, Laurie, my pleasure.'

Laurie had to pause to clear her throat. 'Would you go and ask your boss if he has ever heard of a man called——' and having to swallow before she said his name, 'a man called Tyler Gray.'

'Tyler Gray,' Mei Lai repeated, a smile in her voice as though she suspected a romance had begun in Hong Kong for her friend.

As a minute ticked by, and then two while Mei Lai was away, Laurie began to suspect the worst. But even so she could not stop from hoping with everything in her that when the Chinese girl returned she would be happily singing that her boss did know Tyler Gray, and not, as she was becoming convinced, that he did not.

'Hello, Laurie,' said Mei Lai, and letting Laurie know that when it came to being the biggest greenhorn she was streets ahead of all others, 'Mr Leung has never heard of anybody called Tyler Gray.'

Laurie drove to work that first Monday after her holiday feeling dead inside. Her job, the work, the people she enjoyed, all were at an end, she knew that. If Maruice didn't immediately sack her when she confessed she had lost the ring, then she would resign. She just couldn't continue to work for him with the guilt of that lie inside her.

His reaction when the ring he had entrusted to her wasn't forthcoming she preferred not to think about. But she couldn't tell him the truth, much though Tyler Gray deserved to be found and sent to prison for a couple of years for what he had done.

Oh, he was a real smoothie all right, she thought, hating him with part of her, while the other part just could not be instrumental in having him shut away from society. Mei Lai confirming that her boss had never heard of him cemented that dreadful suspicion that had been spiralling in her while she had been waiting for her to come back with her answer.

The nerve of him! she had thought when the full extent of the con merchant he was had sunk in. The utter nerve! Though wasn't nerve all part of a conman's trade?

It was as clear as crystal to her now why, after having stolen her wallet for pocket money, he hadn't minded using his own money to squire her about. Why should he mind? His outlay was peanuts when up against what he could get for that item of jewellery.

She recalled the way he had said, 'Where the *hell* did you get that?' when he had first seen it. Obvious now was the fact that he had seen straightaway how valuable it was. He had pretended to lose interest in her, he had wanted her huffy so she wouldn't interrupt his thoughts while his devious brain ticked over.

Betsy had said he hadn't been in a sociable mood on the plane to Hong Kong. No wonder! He had wanted peace and quiet during that short flight while he went over his plan looking for flaws. It was the easiest thing in the world for him to read and memorise not only the care-of address on the luggage label, but also Mei Lai's name.

He spoke Cantonese too, Laurie reasoned, only bitterness in her heart for him. With his outsize nerve he had beaten her to Mei Lai's home—that was the reason she hadn't seen more than a glimpse of him at Kai Tak airport—he must have introduced himself to the concierge at Mei Lai's place, discovered Mei Lai wouldn't be back and that she was expecting two visitors from England. Laurie groaned at the way she had innocently told him her friend couldn't make it. Tyler must have seized his opportunity and told the concierge that he was the second English visitor and must have wangled a spare key out of him.

He'd taken an awfully big risk by letting her try to speak to Mei Lai on the telephone that day, she thought. He knew from the concierge, of course, that Mei Lai wasn't at work, but he wasn't to know that the telephone receptionist couldn't speak English. All that pretence too when he had taken the phone from her. Everything had gone his way. He had spoken to the girl in her own language, could have been discussing the weather for all she knew, but it was a certainty they weren't discussing Mei Lai's grandmother's health. The only reason he had been able to dream up that story of the grandmother's failing health was because the concierge must have said something to him about it.

Wanting to crawl into a corner and hide, Laurie parked her car and walked towards the entrance of Craye & Co. She had a few seconds' relief from the certain feeling she was in for a blasting from Maurice when she spotted what looked to be the same opulent car pulled up outside that had been there the very last time she had come through those doors.

Wondering humourlessly if it had been there the whole time, her spirits dropped even lower as memory returned she had thought that car had belong to the big chief himself. Oh, grief, she thought, as she began mounting the stairs, hoping against hope that today of all days wasn't going to be the day she met the boss of the whole outfit for the first time.

Panic hit her at the thought; Harcourt Craye was Anona's brother! That ring had been in his family for years! Her insides like jelly, Laurie reached her landing, and stood there for a moment wanting to run away. Oh God, Harcourt Craye was said to be a tough customer. If he got to hear about the loss of the ring would he be likely to shrug his shoulders and say the ring was Anona's now and it was up to her what she did about it?

Her face pale, she forced herself to go forward, facing what she did not want to face. That even without her brother's interference Anona, if not Maurice, would call the police in, and she, she who had never fallen foul of the law in her life, would have to lie through her teeth if Tyler was to be protected.

She made it to her office, her hands shaking as she opened the door. The door to Maurice's office was closed, she saw, and she had to work hard again not to turn and go running. She had to go in to see Maurice. Go now, she thought, digging her nails into her palms as she steeled herself against that cowardly streak that had her wanting to flee.

Grabbing at a moment of courage, Laurie went towards Maurice's door, swallowing hard as she raised her shaking hand to tap lightly upon it. And then, afraid her courage would desert her before he called come in, she turned the handle, had taken a couple of steps inside before she realised Maurice was not alone.

'I. . . .' The first word of her apology for intruding on him and the tall dark-suited man with his back to her was out before her heart began hammering that she knew him! Knew him even before he turned round. And the gasp that left her when she saw those dark eyes fix on her was one of astonished incredulity. For the man was *Tyler Gray*!

In seconds her colour changed from ashen to scarlet and back to ashen again. All she could think of was that Tyler must get out of here. Desperately she searched for some way to make him go before Maurice connected that they knew each other. She didn't know what he thought he was doing here, but Maurice was no fool and might well connect him some way, somehow, with the loss of that ring.

But her throat had dried. Not one word could she get to leave it as she stared, her eyes riveted on the black-haired man who was looking steadily back at her, those eyes serious now but which she had once seen burning with passion. And as Maurice made a movement to the side of her and she looked to him, she saw he was beaming, and was staggered to learn that her shocks of the last few days weren't over yet.

'Here she is,' said Maurice cheerfully, just as though, she thought, having no intention of making it look as though she knew Tyler, the two of them had been waiting for her. Then when for Tyler's sake she was going to deny that she knew him, 'There's no need to introduce you, is there, Laurie—you've already met the head of the company, haven't you?'

'H-head. . . .' was all her strangled vocal cords would permit.

What was he talking about? Tyler was nothing more than a common crook. Maurice must be going. . . . But Maurice was in there quickly before she could finish the thought, either nervous himself or thinking she was feeling uncomfortable since she had said nothing in greeting to the man he had referred to as the head of Craye & Company.

'Harcourt has just been telling me,' Maurice said, coming in and doing his best to make her feel more at ease in lofty company, while what she was actually doing was gasping that he was referring to Tyler as Harcourt, 'how you took Anona's ring away with you after you found your flat had been broken into. Bad do that,' he inserted. 'But all's well that ends well. Harcourt has given me the ring and,' his face beaming again, 'I just can't wait to see Anona's face tomorrow morning when I give it to her!'

Maurice had the ring! Dumbstruck—what else he had said spinning in her brain—Laurie returned her stare to the man she had known as Tyler Gray. The man who hadn't corrected her the few times she had called him Mr Gray to his face. The man who was staring back at her, showing no remorse that on any of those occasions he could easily have said, 'The name's Craye, not Gray.'

She took her eyes from him to hear that Maurice was still talking, was still doing his best to make her feel at ease and had left the subject of the ring. He was chattering on like a magpie, not giving Tyler a chance to say anything, though by the look of it Tyler seemed happy for Maurice to talk his nervousness out of his system.

Laurie picked up Maurice's hurried speech to hear him saying something that didn't make the least bit of sense to her.

'. . . . Of course I told Harcourt you wouldn't have made off with that very important piece of paper. But with the only finger prints on that file besides Alastair's and mine being yours, everything pointed to you.' It was Maurice's turn to come in for her wordless stare. 'I hope you understand, Laurie, that under the circumstances there was nothing else for it but to have you followed.'

'Followed!' Shock had her finding her voice as she wondered if the trauma she had been through these past hours had turned her brain. What paper was Maurice going on about? And what was it he was saying about fingerprints?

Maurice smiled at her encouragingly, and went on, 'Harcourt tells me you spotted your tail in Hong Kong.' He smiled again. Tyler said not one single word, but just stood there never taking his eyes off her. 'But all that has reached a satisfactory outcome, hasn't it?' said Maurice. 'So we can forget all about it.' He was beaming again as he said, 'Now tell me, Laurie, did you enjoy your holiday? You're looking a little pale.'

Pale or not, it was precisely at that moment that the tremendous shock she had received, first on seeing Tyler there at all, and then on learning that he was not Tyler Gray, but T. Harcourt Craye, loosened its grip. And it was then the terrible anguish she had known began to find an outlet in the wild, furious anger that started to rise up, an anger so fierce there was no way she was going to contain it. It made her deaf to anything else Maurice was saying, had her forgetting what he had said about a file, fingerprints, that she had been followed. All she could remember was Maurice, the ring now in his possession, happily saying, 'So we can forget all about it.'

Just like that she was supposed to forget she had just endured the worst hours of her life! Just like that she was supposed to forget what a living nightmare it had been! Her livid gaze flew to Tyler, the white about her mouth denoting her fine fury. Just like that she was supposed to forget the trauma! Forget she had been ready to lie herself blue in the face for him, risk jail herself for him. Like *hell* she'd forget it!

Rage like none she had ever experienced propelled her forward until she was standing right in front of the man she knew as Tyler. And then as he calmly looked back, his stance so relaxed, even the audacity of a smile looking ready to break as he stared down at her, Laurie's rage spilled over. And there didn't seem at that moment a word bad enough for him, for all he had put her through.

'You—*bastard*!' she hissed, and let go with her right hand, striking his face a terrible blow that cracked round the room, the force of which threatened to break her wrist.

And while both men looked at her, stupefied by her action, that action was just not enough to relieve the violent rage that boiled inside her.

'That was to make me feel better,' she threw at him, and her other hand came cracking up to meet the other side of his face, serving him a matching red mark. 'And that,' she scorned, 'is for having me absolutely demented since I discovered that ring was missing!'

Tyler made a swift grab for her, but he was a second too late coming out of shock of his own, and Laurie wasn't waiting around for anything.

She was at the door, racing through it before either of them had fully recovered, Maurice looking as though he would never recover. Her eyes spitting fire, Laurie charged to the car park, was in her car, too mad to remember how she had got there.

Someone was banging on the car window, wrenching at the locked door handle. She turned her head, saw it was Tyler, heard him shouting at her to open the door.

'Get lost!' she shouted back, her anger not letting up.

She turned the ignition, saw a grim-looking Tyler had gone to stand in front of her car to stop her from going anywhere, and it did nothing at all to sweeten her temper. She had seen him move quickly before and was mad enough as her feet touched the pedals not to care if the weight of all he had on his conscience had slowed him up at all.

Laurie accelerated forward and saw he had lost none of his speed as Tyler, just in time, jumped out of her way.

CHAPTER ELEVEN

LAURIE made it to her flat in record time, and was still fuming when she pulled up. She was so wildly angry that in fact it had passed her notice that the sleek car she had seen outside the entrance of Craye & Co was right there behind her.

She stepped on to the pavement about to shoot indoors. It was then a hand on her arm stopped her. Stopped her and had her looking up to see Tyler hadn't taken many seconds to get to his car and come chasing after her.

'You!' she said scornfully, pulling to get her arm free.

'Yes, me,' said Tyler, his voice, like his expression, uncompromising, the red marks on either side of his face faded.

'I've got nothing I want to say to you,' she spat at him. 'Let go my arm!'

'Not until you've heard what I have to say.' There was nothing she wanted to hear from him either. Hadn't she heard enough from him? She struggled furiously to get her arm free. 'For God's sake,' she could see he was becoming exasperated, but didn't care, 'just give me a hearing!'

'Like hell I'll give you a hearing!' she grunted. And seeing she could struggle all day and he wasn't going to let go the hold he had on her, she brought back her foot and caught his shin bone the most satisfying thwack, and heard him growl as instinctively he loosened his hold.

Laurie wasn't waiting around to inspect the damage. One jerk and she was free, was racing indoors and up the stairs to her flat. She was nearly at the top when she heard footsteps pounding after her, sprinting footsteps that told her she had nowhere near crippled him as he deserved.

She had her flat door open in no time and was half way

through it, but before she could turn to slam it, the tall broad-shouldered figure of Tyler was right there with her, was forcing her into the room, gaining entrance with her. Then he was no longer hurrying. Having gained his objective, Tyler Harcourt Craye turned and closed the door. His eyes showing a forcefulness, a very deliberate attitude, he turned and faced her, the alertness in his eyes at variance with the casual way he leaned against the door.

'Get out of here!' ordered Laurie, her breathing rapid.

'When I'm ready.'

'Get. . . .'

'Shut up,' he countermanded rudely.

'Go to hell!' she blazed.

'Not before you've listened to what I have to say.'

'What you have to say! My God, haven't I heard *enough*! Y. . . .'

'No, you damn well haven't. For a start you haven't heard why. . . .'

'I'm not interested,' Laurie told him hotly. And to prove it she went swiftly to her bedroom with the intention of shutting herself in until he left.

But she had reckoned without his foot being in the way as she went to slam the door on him, had reckoned without seeing that grim determined look on his face that said he was as set in his mind to make her listen as she was determined not to hear.

'Go—away!' she fumed as furiously she tried to get the door shut.

Then she saw any patience in him was at an end when with a muttered imprecation he had kicked the door open, and in the same movement had her under his arm, was carrying her struggling like fury and with a definite movement had dropped her on to the bed.

He held on to her while she endeavoured to sit up. 'Here or in there makes no difference,' he snarled. 'You're going to hear me out, Lauretta Frost, if I have to tie you to the bed!'

'*I will not!*' she shouted, beating at him with her fists as she tried to get away.

'You damn well will,' he told her harshly, grabbing hold of her flailing hands.

'Let—go—of—me,' she panted, hating him afresh that all her struggles were succeeding in doing were making her breathless.

'I'll let you go if you promise to behave yourself,' he ground out, and at her furious impotent glare, 'You hit me once more when I let go of you and I swear by all I hold holy I shall hit you back!'

He meant it too, the woman-battering swine, she could see that. 'A gentleman to the last,' she sneered—then was disgruntled to find the heat of the volcanic temper that had been in her was burning itself out.

Tyler had noted the lessening of her furious anger too. She knew that as his eyes fixed on hers he relaxed his grip, the alert look in those dark eyes telling her he was ready to intensify his hold, set about her most likely, if she so much as moved a muscle.

'All right now?' he asked, his cool enquiry sending her mercury soaring again. 'Are you ready to sit quiet and listen?'

Mutinously she glared at him. He could go to hell, she thought, ready to tell him so. Then she had cause to hate that curiosity in her that chose just that moment to stir itself and have her wondering what it was he had to say that he thought might in any way be a viable explanation for the way he had led her on.

Mulishly she remained silent, but was the first to look away when Tyler, keeping his eyes on her, moved from bending over her to come and sit on the bed beside her, and didn't look to be going to say another word until he was sure she was going to sit quiet and listen.

'I'll sit—because I have no choice,' she muttered. 'But don't think I'm going to believe a word of anything you have to say—nothing is going to whitewash what you've put me through.'

He let go her wrists, his mouth firm. 'Don't judge me until you've heard everything first,' he said quietly, when she had already judged him and found him the most despicable character of all time. 'I didn't mean to make you suffer, but it wasn't until this morning that—certain matters became very clear to me.'

'This morning?' she questioned, her curiosity getting the better of her when she had not meant to contribute one single solitary word more.

'This morning,' he confirmed. 'But to start at the beginning——' He took a long breath, eyed her steadily, then as though impatient to get on, 'You know now that it was I who searched through your case in. . . .'

'And took my wallet—pity for you I had the ring in my bag all the time. That's what you were after, wasn't it?' she inserted as her brain grew active, and anger began to grow again that Anona must have discovered her ring missing *and* who had got it, and asked her brother to retrieve it for her.

'I wasn't looking for the damned ring,' he said shortly, not pleased with her interruption. 'I didn't know you had the blasted thing at that time.'

Laurie threw him a sceptical look that said 'and other fairy tales' which earned her a look from eyes that were starting to glint, warning her to watch it. She ignored his look, mentally declaring she wasn't afraid of him.

'I knew you weren't fully comprehending what Maurice was telling you back at the office,' he resumed, when for all she wasn't afraid of him, Laurie had no comment to make.

'I didn't have to hear anything other than that you weren't Tyler Gray, but T. Harcourt Craye, to know. . . .'

'Maurice was saying,' he cut her off, strangling his 'God

give me strength' look at birth, 'that the final sheet of paper, all Alastair's conclusions on the answer to the metal erosion problem he had worked so solidly on these past months, went missing.'

'*Missing*? Alastair's pap. . . .' Her face paling, her eyes saucer-wide, Laurie looked at him aghast. Anger vanished, incredulity forcing it out as what he was saying sank in. 'No!' she cried, having to accept it. She knew just how vital it was that none of Alastair's findings should get into the wrong hands, and her enmity with Tyler left her. 'Oh no,' she said, her voice hushed.

Then while Tyler was observing her, seeing for himself how shocked she was, she groped, trying to recall what it was Maurice had said. He had said something about fingerprints, she remembered. Something about—about her being—followed! And Laurie was then awash with fresh shock.

'You thought—you thought *I* had it!' she gasped, her senses reeling. 'You *actually* thought *I* had it!'

Whether Tyler thought she was going to start swinging again as he witnessed how the fact she must be the prime suspect had shaken her, she had no idea. But he took hold of her hands, this time in a gentle hold, not knowing she was too amazed to think of hitting anyone.

'I'm sorry, believe me,' he said quietly, his look sincere as he watched the colour return to her face. 'But on the evidence we had then, it could only be you.'

'W-why? How?' she choked.

'You were the only one left alone in the office after Alastair's papers had been put in the safe.'

She couldn't remember being left alone, it was too long ago, though she conceded that she probably had been. 'But I don't have a key to the safe,' she protested—and felt a flutter of anger if that twitch at the corner of his mouth indicated that he had just suppressed a smile.

'Maurice confessed he has left the key with you many

times when he's had to leave the office but has been expecting Alastair to want something from the safe,' he said, adding, 'It wouldn't take long for an industrial spy to take an impression of any key.'

'Industrial spy?' she exclaimed, flabbergasted, gasping anew. 'You think I'm an *industrial spy?*'

'We're getting away from the point,' said Tyler, which was most unsatisfactory from where she was sitting. 'As you know, I think, Alastair contacted me in great excitement once his findings had been safely handed in. Since I had studied physics too, apart from the benefit to the firm, I was almost as excited as he was. Naturally I came straight over.' He broke off, saw he was holding her interest, then said, 'I passed you on my way in.'

'It *was* you I bumped into!' She had no trouble in remembering his rudeness. Oh, if only she had seen his face—she would have known him straight away in China whatever name he chose to call himself, she was sure of it.

'You had such a lot on your mind you weren't alert to where you were going. I remembered that after I'd congratulated Alastair and we went to the safe for him to show me his proved theory.'

'But that final vital paper wasn't there,' Laurie said hoarsely, her thinking power rapid now. 'So you thought, since I appeared to have a lot on my mind, that I. . . .' She couldn't finish, it was too terrible. It forced her to have to remember back nearly four weeks ago to what had been on her mind at the time. It wasn't just her holiday she had been thinking of, she recalled. Anona had seen Maurice giving her that peck on the cheek, and it had worried her.

'I—I wasn't thinking about anything to do with the professor's work,' she said quietly.

'I know,' said Tyler, which lifted her for a moment. That was until she realised she was still the first suspect.

'Yet straight away you thought it was me?'

'Not straight away,' he denied. 'You wouldn't have been allowed anywhere near the paper work if there'd been any doubts about you.' And as though he regretted having to say it, 'But after every item had been taken from that safe, checked and doubled checked, you just had to be the number one suspect.'

Swallowing hard that he could believe anything so diabolical about her, but a streak of fairness in her had admitting that never having met her, not knowing the first thing about her then, maybe he had a right. But what were the others doing while all this was going on? Hadn't Alastair or Maurice, more chums than scientist and boss she had always thought, hadn't they had a good word to say for her?

'Alastair and Maurice believed it too, did they?' she asked dully.

'No,' said Tyler sharply. 'Alastair said he couldn't believe it was you, though you'll appreciate, I'm sure, that because of the hours of labour he'd put in, who had the paper was of lesser concern to him. More especially he wanted that paper back.'

'And Maurice?'

'Never have I heard a more vehement defence,' Tyler told her.

But somehow, in the way he said it, Laurie gained the distinct feeling that Maurice's defence of her had worked against rather than for her. She soon saw why when Tyler went on.

'Maurice was still protesting your innocence when I sent him with Alastair to test the file for fingerprints.' He halted, and while her mind caught up that if there were only three sets of prints on that file and its contents, the other two sets belonging to Maurice and Alastair, it was going to look blacker than ever for her, she saw Tyler was looking at her oddly just before he brought out, 'It was while they were away that Anona appeared, having missed all that had been going on—she'd locked herself in the rest room, from what she said.'

'Oh,' said Laurie, knowing now what was coming.

'I could see she'd been weeping,' he said, which didn't lessen her suspicions as she realised he would never believe her against the sister he was devoted to. 'She told me,' he said slowly, 'that she'd seen Maurice kissing you.'

'It was only a peck,' Laurie said sharply, her self-defence mechanism being activated that there seemed no end to the crimes being laid at her door. 'He'd never done such a thing before. He wouldn't have done so then, only he got a bit emotional—all for love of Anona,' she inserted quickly, 'and how thrilled she was going to be with her birthday present. He'd had a new stone put in her ring—and I'd promised to keep the wretched thing safe for him until today.'

Tyler smiled. 'I know that now,' he said, then proceeded to send a whole gamut of different feelings rioting within her when he said, 'He told me everything a short while ago when I told him he could forget his affair with you because—you were no longer interested in him.'

About to protest that she had never been having an affair with Maurice, she suddenly thought that Tyler had sounded far too confident that she was no longer interested in the man who up until the time Maurice had explained everything, he had been certain she had been having an affair with. That realisation froze any protest she had to make. Oh God, did his confidence stem from the fact that he knew she was no longer interested in any man but him? Did he know she loved him? She just didn't dare risk finding out. She stayed quiet.

Tyler waited for her protest, but when it didn't come, he continued. 'To go back to that vital paper,' he said, when she couldn't remember quite when they had left it, not sure now which was the greatest secret, the paper or her love. 'With Anona believing you were having an affair with her husband, breaking her heart that he'd gone back on his solemn vow, it made all his protestations of your innocence worthless.'

'You believed her?' The hurt in her had the question asked before she realised she was taking him off the subject of the paper again.

'You knew he'd had an affair before?' Tyler countered.

'Yes,' she had to own, condemning herself, she saw, with that confirmation. Wasn't it natural, with his sister being so upset, with him knowing Maurice had been weak once before, that Tyler should give credence to what Anona told him?

'How then should I not believe her?' It was a natural question, but he didn't wait for her to answer. 'With Anona being so upset I knew I'd get nothing sorted about the other business. I called Maurice to take her home, telling him I wanted a word with him later.' Remembering Maurice had been afraid of murder the one and only time he had gone off the rails, Laurie couldn't help but feel for him—but Tyler was going on. 'It took only seconds after they'd gone to get on to the security staff and send one of them round to your flat to keep watch, to follow you if you went out.'

Having had to return to that time some weeks ago, Laurie's memory was fast in waking up. So she hadn't imagined that same car outside her flat as being the same one she had seen at the hospital!

'You thought I would be passing that piece of paper on to my accomplice,' she said stonily. 'A pity your security man found nothing more sinister in my movements than a visit to a sick friend in hospital, wasn't it?' And, her brain alive, 'You remembered that, of course, that day we went to Repulse Bay—that time you changed from being—being a grouch, I think you said.'

'I did,' he agreed. 'The security guard, in plain clothes of course, telephoned me from the hospital. He observed you the whole time you were with your friend. He was able to tell me she spent part of the visit weeping, and that she didn't look at all in any sort of shape to take part in any of the skulduggery that was going on.'

'Well, isn't that nice,' Laurie retorted, and found her acid ignored as, when she was certain nothing else could shock her, he went on:

'He also gave me the tip-off that even if you intended to go straight from the hospital home, it would take you a while to get there.'

There was a question there she had to ask, she saw. But as she saw the question, and the answer, so her temper started to struggle for freedom. She managed to keep control.

'Which gave you ample time to get into my flat and search through my belongings. Have you any idea how nauseated I felt that some strange hand had been poking about in my things?'

'Your feelings at that time were not then my first priority.'

If he was aiming to suggest that somehow his regard for her feelings had changed just a little, then, much as she would like nothing better, she just didn't believe it.

'How disappointing for you that you found nothing!'

'It would have saved me a trip to China if I had.'

'So you joined that tour deliberately to spy on me?' she questioned, seeing now that his seeming to turn up everywhere she went had nothing at all to do with the 'holiday romance' he had appeared not averse to. 'What a bore you must have found it!' Sarcasm wasn't of much help, he didn't even fancy her enough for a holiday flirtation, that much was clear. 'It's a wonder to me you didn't try to join the tour I was on,' she said shortly, still trying now not only to check the anger that was rising but to keep him from seeing the pain in her too. 'It would have saved you chasing around to see what I was up to, wouldn't it? Or better still, why didn't you send your security guard to do your dirty work for you?'

'I was cursing that I couldn't send someone else,' he openly admitted. 'But since I'd been to China on business recently I thought my chances of cutting through red tape, of getting a visa quickly, were better. As for joining the tour you were on, you know as well as I do that a list of the names and addresses of fellow tourists is handed out at the start.'

'And that wouldn't have done, would it?' she put in, trying to overcome the bitterness in her. 'Maurice wouldn't remember if he'd let fall where you live, you couldn't risk that I might know your address. But you did know I might begin to wonder about any T. H. Craye being on the same tour.'

He didn't reply to that. He never would waste his time on the obvious, she thought, as he went on to tell her:

'I didn't know you were touring in China at all until I went from your flat to Anona's home and discovered your holiday arrangements.'

'Anona told you she was filling in for me while I was away?'

'She was in bed when I arrived. Maurice went up soon afterwards. But not before I'd accused him of having an affair with you.'

'Thanks very much!'

He ignored the edge in her comment, though she noted the jut of his jaw as he pressed on, not making excuses for his part in any of it.

'I told him I'd seen a suitcase ready packed in your flat and demanded to know what was going on.'

'You thought....' she broke off as the phone call she had tried to make to Maurice that night shot into her head. 'It was you I spoke with on the phone that night,' she said, and as she remembered his rudeness, her voice became accusing. 'You thought Maurice was my lover, that—that we were going away together!'

'The thought that he was going off with you did cross my mind,' he told her bluntly, not backing away from giving her an answer. 'Though that would have meant he was involved somehow with that missing paper, but for all his weakness in other areas I've always known his honesty in business to be above reproach.'

Which was more than he was saying for hers, Laurie thought sourly. 'He denied we were having an affair, of course, and told you I was off to Hong Kong and China for three weeks?' she questioned, keeping a tight rein on her feelings as her mind switched back to the missing paper. 'You straightaway thought then that I was going to the Far East to meet my accomplice?'

Her answer was a brief nod. 'Maurice told me you were going to stay with a girl who works for one of the companies we deal with out there.'

The woodenness of her front collapsed. 'You thought Mei Lai was implicated,' she gasped, 'her firm?'

'No, I didn't. Ting Yat Electronics aren't in that sort of league. But I had to know who your contacts were. We're in a tough competitive business, I had to know which other firm was employing you, which of our competitors would stoop to such dirty warfare.'

She could see that, but it didn't make her feel any better. She wrenched her hands out of his hold. 'So straight away you booked a flight and followed me.'

'Not straight away,' he denied. 'Though I did have someone take the same flight—you were followed.'

'The bald-headed man!'

'I'm sorry he scared you. I. . . .'

'Scared me? I was petrified! I thought he was after Anona's ring.' And as memory of that sprint back to Mei Lai's returned, 'You pretended you didn't believe I was being followed,' she accused.

'I could hardly confirm it,' he pointed out reasonably.

But she didn't feel in a mood to be reasonable. Though that wasn't the reason a frown puckered her brow. In all the theorising he had expounded, there seemed to her to be something wrong somewhere. She stared at her small bedroom chair without seeing it, feeling within a milimetre of grasping what was wrong.

'What is it?' Tyler asked, seeming, if she didn't know him better by now, to be wanting to help her with whatever it was.

'Something's wrong somewhere with your theory that I'm some Mata Hari,' she said. 'I can't put my finger on it, but. . . .' And suddenly it was there. 'I've got it!' she said, and careless that it was his turn to look mystified, 'I've got it,' she repeated, her brow clearing as she turned to him. 'My arrangements to go to Hong Kong had been made for months.' Relief started to flow. That proved she wasn't some double agent or whatever they were called. 'Don't you see,' she said, wondering why with his brain he hadn't seen it, 'Alastair only stumbled on to his solution for that erosion problem that afternoon—he could have taken another couple of months to crack it as far as I or anyone else knew.' Her face grew animated. 'Don't you see. . . .'

'I see,' said Tyler softly, his eyes resting with a surprisingly gentle look on her, 'just how totally innocent you are. What you've just said proves it.' She had thought it would. And yet, although he had agreed she was innocent of the crime, there was something there that had her doubting. 'You have no idea of the many formulas that safe holds, have you?'

'You're saying—I could have raided the safe, that anyone of our competitors would have paid good money to get their hands on anything I filched?'

So much for him saying he thought she was totally innocent, Laurie thought, wishing, if he really believed that, that he would go. Her temper had cooled, making her too

much aware of him sitting so close to her. She should
have insisted on hearing anything he had to say in the
other room, she thought, only her temper had been so
shot, she hadn't been thinking at all.

'I'm saying I've learned a great deal about you these
last couple of weeks, Laurie,' he said, still speaking softly,
which wouldn't do at all if she was going to find something
in her to show him the door presently with any sign that
he meant nothing to her. 'Everything you've said and
done has all gone to prove you haven't a dishonest bone
in your body. I had further proof this morning when I
went to see Maurice, that to cheat and deceive just isn't
in you.'

Oh God, she wished he wouldn't go on like this! Her
backbone was like water. She couldn't, wouldn't, dared
not look at him. He would soon see she was becoming
putty in his hands. She strove hard for some stiffening, and
found it in a part that hadn't been explained.

'I still don't see why you had to steal my wallet,' she
said, glad to find her voice was firmer than her liquid
spine. Then, 'Oh yes, I do. You wanted me broke so I
couldn't go anywhere.'

He shook his head. 'Time was going on. You'd been in
touch with no one that first week. I wanted you broke so
you would be forced to meet your contact.' His expression
was wry when he added, 'You puzzled me when you asked
me to change your flight without that contact being made.
Either you were throwing a red herring my way—which
meant you'd rumbled me—or you had some other plan in
mind. In either event I hadn't gone all that way, dogged
your heels for a week, just to have my efforts come to
nothing. I'd made too many arrangements to come back
empty-handed.'

'Arrangements? Oh, you mean the tour, your visa. . . .'

'Plus the phone call I made to the head of Ting Yat
Electronics before you'd so much as set foot out of

England.' Her lack of comprehension was so obvious, Tyler allowed himself a smile that was almost a grin. 'I needed to make provision to have your friend Mei Lai out of the way should I find it necessary to move in with you.'

'Mei Lai was in on this too?'

'No, she hasn't a clue what's been going on.'

Laurie saw then just why Mei Lai's boss had insisted she stay the two extra weeks with her grandmother in China. 'Mr Leung agreed to what you wanted—just like that?'

'He's a business man, he was happy to oblige. Especially with the hint of more business coming his way.'

And of course Mr Leung had never heard of Tyler Gray because the head of the company he did business with was called T. Harcourt Craye. Bridge Electrics was just some name Tyler had dreamed up on the spur of the moment.

She saw then that there was no more to be said. Tyler believed in her innocence. Maurice had got the ring back. What more was there to say except goodbye? She moved, intending to get to her feet, then found she couldn't because Tyler seemed to be aware of her every movement and had suddenly placed an arm around her shoulders. The weakness just the feel of him aroused had her fighting hard to remain cool.

'I think we've done that bit, haven't we?' she said as coldly as she could manage. And, hating that her voice betrayed her in that it had gone husky, 'You've explained everything to me and I—I've listened. But now, Ty—Mr Craye, I think you should go. You've now said all you came to say.'

'I have not said all I came to say by any means,' his voice came back firmly as he refused to take his arm from around her.

Fighting like crazy against her need to wilt against him, Laurie strove to find what else it was he had to say, and wasn't surprised she had missed the most important piece of all in this mess, not with her being so much aware of him beside her the whole time.

'Of course,' she said, still trying to shrug off his arm. 'You haven't found that paper yet, have you?' And the stiffening she wanted came to her and with it a coldness of heart as she realised although he had said he believed in her innocence, it was just another lie. 'What are you trying now, Tyler—another seduction scene?' Anger came and she was glad of it. 'Another seduction scene where you think once you've got me as soft in your hands as—as I was that other time I shall tell you where that paper is?'

She had strength to look at him then. She saw his face had hardened, but he still refused to take his arm away. 'Any seduction scene, as you call it, will from here on have nothing to do with that blasted paper,' he said shortly.

But she didn't believe him—she had learned the hard way. Then suddenly, as she glared at him, she saw the hardness in him vanish, saw that weakening smile appear as softly he said:

'The paper had already been found the last time I held you in my arms.'

'Found?' Her anger promptly disappeared. 'But—but I thought you said you'd had everything out of that safe. That. . . .'

'The safe was springcleaned like it had never been springcleaned before.' He smiled the smile that was her undoing. 'It wasn't found in England.' His smile deepened. 'It was found in—Hong Kong.'

'In *Hong Kong*! But—where? Who—who had it?'

She couldn't see why he was enjoying this moment so much as for the second time she saw his ear-to-ear grin. 'My dear Laurie,' he said softly, setting her heart jumping about like a cat on hot bricks, 'you did.'

'*I did!*'

'Not only did you have it, but oh, so innocently you gave it to me that day we were sitting on the sand at Repulse Bay.'

Weakly her voice came this time, as again she said, 'I did?'

His arm still holding her, gently Tyler touched her face. 'Alastair's conclusions were written on the reverse side of that piece of "scrap" Maurice had given you.'

Stunned, Laurie's jaw dropped open. Then as her mind caught up, gasping, she slowly exclaimed, 'The paper with the restaurant address on!' And suddenly it was all too much. She giggled. 'Oh, my sainted aunt!' she breathed. And with that afternoon clear in her mind, that afternoon when he had said 'I love you' without meaning it, 'That's why you were so pleased with yourself. And there was I thinking you were ribbing me because I'd been a bit prim. That's why you said you loved me because at last you could. . . .' her voice began to peter out as the realisation came home that as a person she was of very little interest to him, '. . . . so you could leave and—and forget I ever existed.'

She wanted him to go. She didn't want him to see her tears, tears that were welling up from the very heart of her that with his business satisfactorily completed, he had left. He hadn't hung around once he had got that paper, had he?

'Never could I forget your existence,' he salved her pride, but shattered her altogether as he went on, 'When I told you I loved you, I meant exactly that.'

Her eyes flew to his in disbelief. 'You were joking,' she said hoarsely, scarlet flags in her cheeks.

'I meant it to sound that way,' he admitted gently. 'It had only just then struck me how much you'd come to mean to me. The words were there, and had to be released. I just couldn't hold them in. I knew then I loved everything about you—not least your proud loyalty to the company you worked for—my company.'

Striving for breath, her heart racing overtime, Laurie stared and stared, and just couldn't believe it.

'Th-there was nothing to stop you from releasing it,' she said—and straightaway wished she hadn't. Tyler was too quick not to see from those words that since she wasn't putting up objections to him being in love with her, then he must see it as a very clear indication of what her feelings for him were.

It did nothing to restore her equilibrium to have the feel of his hand once more on her skin as he turned her face to him. Nor did it help her to hear him say, 'My lovely girl!' to feel his lips against hers in a feather-light kiss, before he went on, 'There was still the matter of Anona's ring in the way.'

'You—er—thought Maurice had given it to me?' she asked, trembling, a feeling of wanting to believe he loved her at odds with the impossibility of it ever being true.

'I got the shock of my life when I saw a ring in your possession I well remembered my mother wearing. The last time I'd seen it was when I handed it over to Anona. It confirmed for me that you must be having an affair with her husband. Why else would he give it to you?' He set her heart thundering again by once more caressing her lips with his. 'Though I knew from the way you'd returned my kisses that you couldn't be in love with him.'

'I—er——' she began, not at all sure what she wanted to say. Then, although she knew she was being more foolish than she had ever been in her whole life, she just had to meet him half way, just in case—in case he wasn't leading her on with his talk of loving her. 'I—I came out of the bedroom—that last night—to tell you all about that ring.' She coughed, her nerves all screwed up. 'I—er—wanted you to know I wasn't having an affair with anyone—before I—er—left the next day.'

'And that was when I saw you looking, so clean, scrubbed and adorable, I felt compelled to tell you some of the thoughts that were going through my head.'

'But—you—didn't.' Hope reached a peak as she smiled—and he smiled back.

'Our lips met and that was it,' he said softly. 'All thought went from my head but that I had to hold you in my arms,' his voice faded, 'like this,' he breathed.

There was nothing feather-light about the kisses that assaulted her lips then. As though he had been starved of the feel of her lips beneath his, Tyler took more and yet more, holding her close as he felt her response, moving with her, their arms encircling each other until they were lying on top of her bed, the narrowness of it having nothing to do with the way they stayed close.

'My dear love,' he whispered then their lips broke apart and they lay just staring into each other's eyes.

'Is it true?' Laurie said huskily, knowing fate couldn't be so cruel as to plummet her to the depths if it wasn't.

'That I love you, my dear heart?' he asked softly. 'Yes, my darling, it's true. It was growing in me that day you were lost. It was the only time I lost track of you. I knew you hadn't arranged to meet up with anyone when Betsy eventually turned up and told me it was an unscheduled stop. I began to grow concerned for you when the minutes ticked by and no Lauretta Frost. But I had no idea then why I should be worried that you must be lost.'

'It was the first time you called me Laurie,' she whispered.

'I forgot in my concern that I wasn't supposed to know you by the name Maurice and Alastair called you by,' said Tyler, his fingers gently tracing the outline of her mouth. Then, kissing those lips he couldn't resist, 'I love you with everything that's in me, my dear love. Love you so much it tore the heart out of me to leave you in Hong Kong.'

'Why did you?' she asked, her eyes shining as she looked at him. 'You could have told me about the missing paper, explained that it was because of that that you stole my wallet.'

'As I remember it,' he said, his voice gently teasing, 'you were in no mood to listen to explanations.' Laurie remembered the way she had sent his case skidding out of the bedroom, but had little time to regret her action, for Tyler was saying seriously, 'That had nothing to do with the reason I left, left without declaring my love.' And as her face too grew serious, he told her, 'I needed to have that ring returned to its rightful owner. Needed to see my brother-in-law to tell him that if he so much as looked sideways at you again. . . .' He broke off, his eyes adoring on her face. 'I needed to get all that cleared up before I asked you to marry me.'

'Marry you!' Laurie just hadn't got that far in her thinking.

'You are going to marry me, aren't you?' Unable to believe what her eyes were telling her, she saw in the stirrings of aggression in him, that he must be in some doubt that she wouldn't rush to say yes. 'You do love me, don't you? You must,' he urged. 'Say that you do.'

'I—er—think I must do,' she said demurely, wanting to do nothing but kiss that mouth that was so near to her own. 'I was ready to cover for you this morning, lie my head off to the police and everyone else when I told them I'd lost that ring.'

'You would have done that for me?' he asked incredulously.

'I love you,' she said simply.

'Oh, my love!' And it seemed then that he had the same need to feel her lips against his. He kissed her long and lingeringly. But at last he pulled back. 'Oh, my dear, dear love,' he said hoarsely. Then, 'And you will marry me?' he asked.

'Oh yes!' said Laurie, and eagerly met his lips again when he once more claimed her mouth.

Delighting in her, Tyler told her he had no idea she would be as frantic as she had been when she discovered the loss of the ring. 'I didn't know you were only keeping it so Anona shouldn't see it before her birthday,' he said, a tenderness in him she had never dreamed of. 'I thought if anything you'd be as mad as hell that I'd pinched it—that was if you'd discovered I'd taken it before I met you at Gatwick.'

'Gatwick?'

'I fully intended to meet you off your plane,' he told her. 'I had a few hours, I thought, to sort Maurice out before you landed. But the best laid plans, etcetera. Anona and Maurice had chosen that time to have an extra long weekend away without leaving word of where they were going.'

'I know, I tried to phone Maurice to stop him from worrying on Monday when I didn't turn up.'

'You weren't going to go in today?'

'I was going to go to Milton Keynes looking for you,' Laurie said, explaining the whole of the nightmare she had been through.

'My God,' Tyler muttered when she had finished, 'to think I, who would never harm a hair on your head, put you through all that!'

'It doesn't matter,' she said, shrugging off what had been an awful time for her, and trying to take the terrible look of remorse from off his face. 'Not harm a hair on my head,' she teased. 'Would you really have hit me if I'd hit you again?'

His smile broke delighting her. 'Kissing you was more what I had in mind,' he breathed softly—and held her close to his heart as he proceeded to do so.

FREE!
Romance Treasury

A beautifully bound, value-packed, three-in-one volume of romance!

Romance Treasury

An exciting opportunity to collect treasured works of romance! Almost 600 pages of exciting romance reading in each beautifully bound hardcover volume!

You may cancel your subscription whenever you wish! You don't have to buy any minimum number of volumes. Whenever you decide to stop your subscription just drop us a line and we'll cancel all further shipments.